Look what p...
Br...

"Brenda Jackson writes romance that sizzles and characters you fall in love with."
—Lori Foster, *New York Times* bestselling author

"Jackson's trademark ability to weave multiple characters and side stories together makes shocking truths all the more exciting."
—*Publishers Weekly*

"Ms. Jackson has proven once again why she is truly one of the Divas of romance."
—*Romance In Color*

"Jackson's novels are an armchair matchmaker's dream."
—*Romance Reader*

"*The Midnight Hour* is a roller-coaster read of passion, intrigue and deceit."
—Sharon Sala, *New York Times* bestselling author

"With her inimitable style, Ms. Jackson has created another rip-roaring, seductively sensual love story that is sure to take the romance-reading community by storm. As always, her standard of excellence is evident in every scintillating page of *Fire and Desire*."
—*RT Book Reviews*

Blaze

Dear Reader,

I've been anxiously waiting to be able to write Duan Jeffries's story—and I'm thrilled to introduce him in my very first Blaze novel. My readers first met the Jeffries clan when Reggie Westmoreland fell in love with Olivia Jeffries in my Silhouette Desire book titled *Tall, Dark...Westmoreland!* Since then, I couldn't get Olivia's two older brothers, Duan and Terrence, out of my mind. Terrence made his debut in my Kimani novel *Temperatures Rising,* and now, finally, it's Duan's turn.

I love writing about men who are smooth, suave and seductive. And of course they have to be gorgeous as well. With Duan I threw in an additional element—he's a great multitasker. He can get his girl with one hand and take down the bad guys with the other. I saw him as a perfect fit for Kim Cannon, a free-spirited soon-to-be doctor, who thought she knew exactly what she wanted until Duan came along.

I hope you enjoy reading Duan and Kim's story. Be sure to check out the Blaze list for upcoming books about the hot guys who work with Duan in the Peachtree Private Investigative Firm.

I love hearing from my readers. You can contact or e-mail me at WriterBJackson@aol.com.

All the best,

Brenda Jackson

Brenda Jackson

SPONTANEOUS

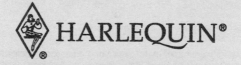

TORONTO • NEW YORK • LONDON
AMSTERDAM • PARIS • SYDNEY • HAMBURG
STOCKHOLM • ATHENS • TOKYO • MILAN • MADRID
PRAGUE • WARSAW • BUDAPEST • AUCKLAND

Recycling programs
for this product may
not exist in your area.

ISBN-13: 978-0-373-79542-0

SPONTANEOUS

ABOUT THE AUTHOR

Brenda Jackson is a die "heart" romantic who married her childhood sweetheart and still proudly wears the "going steady" ring he gave her when she was fifteen. Because she's always believed in the power of love, Brenda's stories always have happy endings. In her real-life love story, Brenda and her husband of thirty-eight years live in Jacksonville, Florida, and have two sons.

A *New York Times* bestselling author of more than seventy romance titles, Brenda is a retiree from a major insurance company and divides her time between family, writing and traveling. Be sure to visit her Web site at www.brendajackson.net.

Books by Brenda Jackson

SILHOUETTE DESIRE
1850—TAMING CLINT WESTMORELAND
1874—COLE'S RED-HOT PURSUIT
1911—QUADE'S BABIES
1928—TALL, DARK...WESTMORELAND!
1958—ONE NIGHT WITH THE WEALTHY RANCHER
1975—WESTMORELAND'S WAY
2000—HOT WESTMORELAND NIGHTS

To my husband, the love of my life
and my best friend, Gerald Jackson, Sr.

To everyone who enjoys reading
a Brenda Jackson novel, this one is for you!

Happy is the man that findeth wisdom,
and the man that getteth understanding.
—*Proverbs* 3:13

1

My brother has hit gold.

That thought ran through Duan Jeffries's mind while he stood on the sidelines and watched Terrence "Holy Terror" Jeffries escort his bride, Sherri Griffin Jeffries, around the huge ballroom as they thanked the numerous guests for attending their wedding.

From the moment Duan had met Sherri, he'd known she was the one woman who could make his younger brother happy. Just being in their presence was to feel the love radiating between them. And even though he was a downright cynical bastard when it came to the notion of true love, the two of them had made him somewhat of a believer.

The same held true for his sister, Olivia, and the man she'd married last year, Senator Reggie Westmoreland. That was definitely another love match. So okay, two cases weren't bad. He shifted his glance across the room to his father and the woman by his side and chuckled inwardly. All right, he would make that three cases. His father had finally married his devoted administrative assistant a few months back. Duan didn't know any man who deserved the love of a good woman more than Orin Jeffries, especially after all the hell the mother of his three offspring put him through.

Not wanting to think about the woman who'd given birth to him, the same one who'd deserted her husband and three children when Duan was twelve, Terrence ten and Libby three, he glanced at his watch, feeling tired and edgy. He had arrived in Chicago yesterday and come straight from the airport to the church, just in time to make the rehearsal dinner.

A private investigator, for the past three months he'd been working practically around the clock trying to gather enough evidence to hand over to an attorney friend who was convinced a man he was representing had been wrongfully accused of murder. It had been a hard case to crack and even harder to deliver the news that it was the man's wife who'd set him up. With the evidence needed to clear the man of all charges, Duan had taken off from Atlanta on a direct flight to Chicago.

He glanced at his watch. He had another hour or so before the wedded couple headed for O'Hare and a two-week honeymoon in Paris. After they departed he would go up to his hotel room, get out of his tux and change into something more comfortable and…

Do what?

He didn't have any immediate plans. Word had gotten around that some of Reggie's brothers and cousins were hosting a card game later tonight in one of their rooms. He wasn't surprised. He had known most of the Westmorelands from his high-school years in Atlanta and had rekindled friendships with them since Reggie had married Libby. The one thing he knew about them was that they liked to gamble, and their game of choice was poker.

Duan decided to pass after remembering what happened the last time he'd played with them. When the game ended he'd been three hundred dollars poorer.

If not poker, then what else was there to do?

He shifted his gaze to the woman standing across the room talking to the bride's parents. Immediately, he felt a primitive thrumming heat run through him. Kimani Cannon. He would definitely love to *do* her.

She was the best friend of the bride and he had been attracted to her from the first moment they'd been introduced a few months ago at Terrence and Sherri's engagement party in the Keys. He had immediately picked up on the strong sexual chemistry flowing between them, and the look Kimani had given him promised that they would hook up later to wear out somebody's sheets. But before they could make that happen, he'd received an important tip on a case he was working and had to leave.

She was definitely nice to look at with her dark, sultry eyes, a cute pixie nose and full and shapely lips. He particularly liked the mass of dark brown spiral curls that crowned her creamy cocoa-colored face.

She was downright sexy from the top of her head past those shapely curves and gorgeous legs to the soles of her feet. And speaking of feet, he had a weakness when it came to women in high heels, especially if they had the legs for them, which she did. And the strapless satin baby-blue maid-of-honor dress that hit below the knees looked damn good on her, but he'd much prefer seeing her naked. He wanted to find out if his dreams came close to the real thing.

He took a sip of his drink and continued to watch her. Lust after her was more like it. And it wasn't helping matters when all kind of wicked fantasies danced around in his head. He could envision doing something hot, naughty and X-rated with her—like locking himself between her legs and staying there until there wasn't anything left to give or take.

His fingers tightened on the stem of the wineglass, not sure what part of her he enjoyed staring at the most, and quickly decided he liked everything about her. Even from across the room she stirred his blood, fired his senses and made him think about hot sex under silken sheets.

He dragged in a deep breath and reached up to loosen his tie, which suddenly felt tight. Hell, even his briefs were restricting. And the rumble deep in his gut, trickling down toward his groin, could only mean one thing. After a six-month abstinence, he needed to get laid. And he wondered if the woman across the room would in any way be accommodating.

No sooner had that thought worked its way into his mind then she glanced over in his direction. Their gazes locked and the chemistry flowing between them thickened, stirred and escalated. Heat shimmered in the air and then she broke eye contact with him. Placing her wineglass on the tray of a passing waiter, she headed out of the ballroom. He watched, mesmerized by the sway of her hips and those gorgeous legs in high heels.

Suddenly, he felt his feet moving to follow her.

KIM RELEASED A DEEP breath as she walked down the hall that led to the room the bridesmaids had used earlier to dress in. She heard footsteps behind her and didn't have to turn around to know the identity of the person following her.

Duan Jeffries.

There was something about him that made her immediately think of sex, sex and plenty more sex. In that brief moment they'd made eye contact in the ballroom, she had detected the raw hunger within him, a need that was both possessive and magnetic, and it had drawn her to him, filled her with a desire to take him on right now.

Due to budget cuts at the hospital where she worked as an E.R. nurse, she hadn't had much of a social life lately. Seeing Duan made her realize just how much she longed for some skin-to-skin contact. Licking him from head to toe would be a good start, but she figured they wouldn't have enough time for that. A quickie would have to do.

She'd known the instant she met him four months ago that they would eventually get together. The vibes had been strong and she was disappointed when he'd left the Keys unexpectedly. The only reason she hadn't initiated jumping his bones after the rehearsal dinner last night was because she and Sherri had planned to hang out with her cousins one last time in Sherri's hotel room.

A shiver of anticipation flowed through her body when she came to a stop in front of the room. Without looking over her shoulder, she turned the knob, pushed opened the door and stepped inside.

It was only when she heard the sound of the door closing and the lock clicking in place behind her that she turned to stare up into what had to be the most gorgeous dark eyes any man could possess. And then there were the perfect angles, seamless planes and sensuous lines that made up an impressive and sinfully handsome face.

He took a step closer and she sucked in a quick breath when she felt his erection poke into her belly. She wasn't sure who made the first move after that. It wasn't really important. All that mattered was the mouth that swooped down, taking hers with a hunger that she reciprocated.

When she met his tongue with her own, he deepened the kiss and then it was on. Something frantic broke within her, within them, and a need as raw as it could get took over.

She felt his hand lifting her dress. The sound of silk rustling against silk inflamed her mind, and when those same hands made contact with the apex of her thighs, not even her panties were a barrier against the busy fingers that sought and found an easy opening.

And then those fingers were moving through the curls, beyond the folds, stirring her wetness and massaging her clit. She moaned at the invasion as well as the pleasure, and instinctively reached for his fly and eased down the zipper. Quickly inserting her hand beneath the elastic waistband of his briefs, she gripped the engorged hardness of his sex. He pulled his mouth from hers and released a guttural groan, and the primitive sound was something she understood and identified with.

"Condom." He said that one word in a ragged breath and she relinquished her hold on him so he could fish into the pockets of his pants for his wallet. He pulled out a square packet.

She shifted her gaze from the condom to his erection, jutting proudly from a dark thatch of curls. The head of his shaft was big and smooth, and the veins running along the sides were thick.

Heat burning in every part of her body, she watched as he sheathed himself with such ease and accuracy that she figured he'd done this numerous times. When that task was completed, he glanced up and the eyes that stared at her nearly scorched her skin and made her regret they only had time for a quickie. Leisurely savoring every inch of him was something she would just love doing. But for now she would take what she could get. Leaning up on tiptoe, she pressed her moist lips against his.

His mouth immediately captured hers, kissing her hungrily, and she felt him tug her dress up. She had a feeling this mating would be a quickie like nothing she'd ever experienced.

He lifted her, cupping her hips in his hands, and she instinctively wrapped her legs around him. Like radar his engorged sex found its mark and he pushed forward, sliding between her wet folds. The size of him stretched her, filled her to capacity. And it seemed his erection got larger as he delved deeper and deeper…pressing her back against the wall.

He paused, as if he wanted to experience the feeling of being embedded within her, and in protest her inner muscles clamped down hard on him, then let go, repeating the process a few times. He snatched his mouth from hers, threw his head back and released a massive growl.

To her satisfaction he began moving, pounding in and out of her in a rhythm that matched the beat of her heart. She hoped and prayed the room on the other side of the wall was empty. She would hate for anyone to want to investigate what all the noise was about.

She felt his every thrust all the way to her toes—toes that were curled around his waist at that very moment. His erection was throbbing inside her with the intensity of a volcano about to erupt.

He leaned down and imprisoned her mouth again, kissing her hungrily. Was there anything this man couldn't do perfectly? She moaned and worked her body against his, meeting him stroke for stroke, thrust for thrust.

She pulled back from the kiss, needing to see him, to look into his face, to know he was feeling the same things she was. Pure feminine satisfaction poured through her at the intense look on his features that told her he was. And if that didn't convince her, then his thrusts did. They were powerful, each one an accurate hit, centering on her G-spot with clear-cut precision and a mastery that had her panting. And still he thrust deeper, pounded harder.

And then she felt it, the first signs of the explosive tension building inside her and inside him, as well. His muscular thighs began quivering with an intensity that she felt through his tuxedo pants. And then he let out a deep moan followed by a release that triggered her own eruption, and he clamped his mouth on hers to quell her scream.

Their tongues tangled once again and she was devoured by his greedy mouth. Giving in to pent-up passion and bridled lust, she wrapped her arms around him as he continued to rock into her, as if taking her this way was his due. His every right.

And at that moment, it was.

DUAN SHOVED HIS SHIRT into his pants as he glanced over at Kimani. She was smoothing her dress over those luscious curves. The woman was something else, and even now, while aftershocks of his orgasm were still flitting through his system, his body was aching for more. What was it about her that made him into one greedy ass where her body was concerned?

He breathed in deeply. The scent of sex mingled with the perfume she was wearing had to be filling her nostrils the way it was his. He liked the aroma. When she reached up and ran fingers through her curls to bring order back to her hair, he thought she looked simply beautiful.

He shook his head. He'd just made out with the maid of honor at his brother's wedding. Hell, they were right down the hall from the reception.

"We need to move quickly if we want to be there when Terrence and Sherri leave," she said, slipping into the shoes she had discarded earlier. Those high heels he liked so much.

He knew it was a stupid thought, but the only place he could imagine being at the moment was right here with her. "And just what will happen if we're not there?" he asked.

She glanced up at him with that *duh* look. "Everyone will wonder where we are. Have you forgotten that you're the best man and I'm the maid of honor?"

He wished he could forget if it meant another round with her. This was not a good time to tell her they'd probably already been missed. There might not be anyone keeping tabs on her, but he was certain Libby would have noticed his disappearing act by now. When it came to him and Terrence, his sister didn't miss a thing. Getting married hadn't changed that about her.

"You look nice in your tux, by the way."

He met her gaze and couldn't help but smile. He thought she had a pair of gorgeous eyes. "And you look good in your dress. But can I be honest with you about something?"

"Yes."

"I really wanted to see you naked."

He waited, fully expecting her to say something like this had been one of those done deals and there wouldn't be a next time so he could chalk it up as a missed opportunity. Instead, she strolled over to him, reached up to straighten his tie, then stood on tiptoe and leaned closer to whisper, "That can be arranged. I'm in Room 822."

She then slipped out of his reach, and after tossing a saucy smile over her shoulder, she unlocked the door and walked out.

KIM HEARD HER NAME being called the moment she reentered the ballroom. She glanced over and saw Sherri heading toward her. She was so excited for her best friend and truly believed she and Terrence would be happy together.

"And just where did you slip off to?" Sherri was asking. "I've been looking for you."

Kim threw her head back and laughed. "You mean your husband finally let you out of his sight? Unbelievable."

She and Sherri shared a smile and then Sherri said, "Yes, but only for a minute." Her expression turned serious. "Promise me that you're going to celebrate your good news."

Kim thought about the official letter she had received a couple of days ago. The one informing her she'd been accepted into medical school. "I promise that I will celebrate."

She'd always wanted to become a doctor, but her parents had split in her senior year of high school, which made money tight. Out of spite, her poor excuse for a father had emptied the savings account her mom had set up to defray the cost of college. As a result Kim had to resort to student loans and eventually had to settle on a master's degree in nursing.

She found being a nurse rewarding and was dedicated to the profession, but now it was time to move on and pursue her dream to become a doctor.

Her gaze shifted from Sherri as she caught sight of Duan across the room. Just like she'd told him earlier, he looked good in his tux. On some men a tuxedo looked only so-so, but on Duan it was spine-tingling sexy. Definitely eye candy of the sweetest kind. As if he felt her watching him, he glanced over at her and she tilted her head and smiled.

Sherri noticed the exchange and lifted a brow. "Now, isn't that strange?"

Kim broke eye contact with Duan and turned back to Sherri. "What is?"

"Terrence was searching for Duan at the same time I was looking for you. Imagine that."

Kim shrugged, trying to keep a straight face. "Yes, imagine that."

"You know what I think?" Sherri was grinning.

"Haven't a clue."

Her friend gave her an assessing glance. "I think you've started celebrating already."

DUAN STOOD OFF to the side and watched the newlyweds leave amidst a shower of rice and well-wishes. He took a long drink of his champagne and kept his gaze on Kim, while at the same time pretending interest in the conversations going on around him.

He had already turned down an invitation from Lucas McCoy and Stephen Morales, Terrence's close friends from his college days, to join them and their wives for a night out on the town. And as predicted, the Westmorelands were hosting a poker game in one of their suites.

"You sure you don't want to join us later, Duan?" Stone Westmoreland asked. Duan and Stone had been in the same softball league while growing up and had played football together in high school.

"I'm positive," he said, noting the exact moment Kim began walking toward an exit door. "I had a rough week and need to get to bed early."

Most of what he said was true. No one needed to know that the bed he would be getting into wasn't his.

He exchanged conversation with Stone and the other Westmorelands for a few minutes and then bid everyone a farewell and a safe return home. Like him, most of them would be checking out of the hotel sometime tomorrow. Placing his empty champagne glass on a table, he picked up his pace as he headed toward the elevators.

KIM GLANCED AROUND her hotel room and saw the bottle of champagne Sherri had ordered earlier sitting in a bucket of ice. She hadn't told anyone but Sherri about her acceptance into medical school at the University of California, San Francisco.

She had a couple months to accept their offer. She had applied to three other universities and would wait to hear from them before making a decision.

She smiled as she kicked off her shoes. She was very much aware that Duan had been watching her when she'd left the reception, which meant he was probably on his way up. The quickie earlier had relieved some of the sexual tension between them but not all of it. She had issued the invitation to complete what they'd started, so she had no problem with him taking her up on it.

She liked him, and after what happened earlier, she liked him even more. Even with a limited amount of time he hadn't been a selfish lover. She couldn't say the same for the last guy she'd dated, a surgeon at the hospital. He'd left a lot to be desired.

Kim walked over to the window to take in the view of Lake Michigan. Several small fishing vessels were out on the lake, as well as a number of other boats in various sizes. It was so beautiful she could just stand there a while and watch. Her mother had planned to come to the wedding with her, but had called two days ago and said something had come up and she wouldn't be able to make it. She would have enjoyed being here.

At the thought of her mother, Kim shook her head. She'd been forced to tell a lie to her mom and Aunt Gertrude. She loved the two women to death and they meant well, but recently Aunt Gert had submitted Kim's name to the producers of the reality show *How to Find a Good Man*. That was a bit too much. And when Aunt Gert's essay had won and Kim had been selected as a contestant, she'd come up with the only plausible reason to turn down what her mother and aunt thought was a golden opportunity. Kim had convinced them she'd found a good man on her own.

She turned at the sound of the knock on the door. In a way she had found one, at least for this weekend. A sense of heated anticipation gripped her and she inhaled deeply, more than ready to enjoy another round of hot, heavy and mind-blowing sex.

And this time there wouldn't be any time restraints.

KIM OPENED THE DOOR and immediately heat began stirring through every part of her body. She took a step back when he entered the room.

"Would you like a drink, Duan?"

The smooth smile that formed on his lips made Kim's nipples harden.

"No, thank you," he said, stepping closer.

"In that case…"

She reached up and placed her arms around his neck, going straight for his mouth. In response, turbulent emotions consumed her and made her deepen the kiss the same time he did.

She felt him moving, walking her backward, and when the bed hit her legs she pulled away to break from the kiss. Kim glanced up at him and saw the taut lines of his jaw and the moist sheen of his lips. And then she felt his hand working its way to her back to ease down her zipper. He tugged her dress down her body, right along with her bra. The man knew what he was after. He'd said he wanted to see her naked and wasn't wasting any time getting her that way.

He then proceeded to use both hands to cop a feel of her bare breasts. The moment the pad of his thumbs came in contact with the budded nipples, she felt the crotch of her panties get wet.

His gaze caught hers just moments before he leaned forward and captured a nipple between his lips, savoring it as if it were the best thing he'd ever tasted. He sucked aggressively. Licked profusely. Hard. Hungrily. Moments later he switched to the other breast.

When Kim thought she couldn't handle any more, she felt herself being lowered to the bed, felt the mattress and thick bedcovers beneath her back. He threw his leg over her middle and she moaned at the feel of the material of his pants rubbing against her inner thigh. When she was totally convinced his mouth was about to push her over the edge he released her nipple, lifted his head and met her gaze.

"You have nice breasts," he said in a deep, husky voice.

"Glad to know you like them," she responded, reaching up and brushing her fingers against the length of his jaw.

Someone once said you could tell the strength of a man by his jawbone. If that was the case then Duan Jeffries was the equivalent of Samson. He certainly had a lot of sex appeal.

"We need to get you out of the rest of your clothes," he said, slowly sliding his hands down her body and then back up again, letting his fingertips gently caress her skin, sending heated bliss wherever he stroked.

Kim's pulse rate increased and she dragged air into her lungs as the feel of his touch tormented her flesh. She eased herself up in the bed and he moved to give her room while she removed her stockings, tossing the items aside. She was completely naked except for her panties. And when she leaned back on her elbows and lifted her hips off the bed with a bold unmistaken invitation in her eyes, he reached out and slid her panties down her thighs and legs.

Duan pulled in a deep heated breath as he let his gaze roam over Kim's naked form. Something within him had driven his desire to see her this way and he was not disappointed.

Before he realized what she was doing, she had eased off the bed to kneel in front of him and was sliding down his zipper. She then tugged down his pants and briefs and he stepped out of them. Tossing the pieces of clothing out of the way, she leaned back on her haunches and tilted her head to look up him and smile. "I wanted to do this earlier but time wouldn't allow it."

He pulled in a deep breath when her tongue began licking him from top to bottom and front to back. She then opened her mouth and greedily slid him inside, letting her tongue wrap around his head and then the length of his entire manhood.

His breath caught and he wondered if he would ever be able to breathe again. The sensations were so powerful he could have died right then and there. He'd been given head before, but never with such bold deliberation. And there was a sweetness to her lips that even extended to this.

He threw his head back and growled as she worked her mouth and tongue over his rod. The sight of her on her knees with him fully planted inside her mouth, bobbing her head up and down while her hands played gently with his balls, had his erection throbbing to an almost explosive state. He reached down and grabbed hold of a fistful of her hair to hold her mouth still when the unbearable pleasure intensified. Every cell in his body seemed electrified.

His nerve endings were stretched to the limit and the sensations firing through him shuddered deep in his gut.

When he felt himself almost pushed over the edge, he grabbed her chin and pulled his rod out of her mouth. Ignoring her whimper of disappointment, he lifted her into his arms and quickly crossed back to the bed and placed her on it. He came down with her, and before she could straighten her body, he was there pushing her backward. His hands grabbed hold of her hips and his head went between her legs. Now it was time for his tongue to pleasure her.

His fingers parted her folds, and the moment his tongue slid inside her and he was introduced to her taste, a rush of new sensations surged through him, made him clasp her hips tighter to bring her closer to his mouth. His tongue moved frantically inside her and he knew the exact moment he found what he was seeking.

"Duan!"

He withdrew his tongue and let the tip play with her clit. His lips then came together and greedily devoured it. He had to hold her down with his hands when she began moving frantically beneath his mouth as he savored her unique taste of honey.

She shuddered just seconds before she screamed. It was only after the last spasm passed through her body that he loosened his hold on her and pulled back to retrieve a condom from his wallet.

He sheathed himself and moved back toward the bed to find her still stretched out in that same position, as inviting as any woman could be.

That pose made him ease onto the mattress on all fours, like a lion capturing his prey, and when he had straddled her, effectively pinning her beneath him, he met her gaze. He leaned in and captured her mouth at the same moment that he slid inside her, not stopping until he was buried deep.

And then he began making love to her, deciding there would be nothing quick in their mating this time around.

2

DUAN OPENED HIS EYES and squinted against the bright sunlight flowing in through the hotel-room window. It was at that moment he felt the soft feminine naked body resting against him, his front spooning her backside.

A shiver of pleasure flowed through him when he remembered everything that had happened—all he'd done over the past fourteen-plus hours. And he wasn't feeling one moment of regret. In fact, he felt electrified in a way he'd never felt before. Kim had satisfied a fierce need inside him. Making love to her had been everything he'd wanted, and more.

She had met him on every level and together they had shared climax after magnificent climax. But for some reason what they'd shared was a lot more than sex. She had managed to tap into a Duan Jeffries few people saw. The one who longed not to be so disciplined. The one who didn't necessarily want to be a good guy *all* the time.

Growing up he'd had no choice. He was the oldest and was expected to set a good example for Terrence and Olivia. His mother had caused his father enough scandal, and Orin Jeffries hadn't needed his oldest son to follow in his wife's footsteps. So he had done everything right. He had gotten the best grades in school and had gone into law enforcement after college to keep the bad guys off the street. In a way his occupation as a private investigator was still doing that. He enjoyed his work. He loved preserving the peace and making sure those who broke the law were put behind bars.

But still...

It had been fun slipping off in the middle of his brother's wedding reception for a quickie. And if that hadn't been shameful enough, before Terrence and Sherri could make it to the airport for their honeymoon, he had come up to Kim's room, driven with a desire to see her naked and to engage in more sex. Shameful to some but total pleasure for him.

He was simply enthralled and could only wonder what there was about Kim that made him respond to her with a spontaneity that he found disconcerting as well as fascinating. What was there about her that dared him to become a risk taker?

His thoughts were interrupted when she shifted in sleep, snuggling her luscious backside even closer to him. Already his rod was awake, and the damn greedy bastard was stretching. It obviously liked the feel of Kim's bare bottom pressed against it.

He suppressed the urge. For some reason he didn't want to do anything more than just lie there and hold her, share the essence of her heat.

When he draped his arms across her middle she snuggled closer into him. He liked the feel of having her there, and with that thought firmly planted in his mind, he closed his eyes and joined her in sleep.

"WHAT TIME DO YOU plan to check out today, Kim?"

Kim looked up from her breakfast plate. They had awakened a short while ago, and after taking a shower they'd ordered room service for breakfast. Now, wearing the complimentary bath robes provided by the hotel, they were eating in bed.

"I asked for a late checkout," she replied. "That means I won't be leaving before two. What about you?"

"I asked for a late checkout, as well. My plane doesn't fly out until five and that will give me plenty of time to get to O'Hare."

"I don't fly out until six. Want to share a taxi to the airport?" she asked, taking a sip of coffee.

His smile sent a warm feeling all through her in a way even the coffee hadn't done. "Yes, that will work."

She resumed eating. She would be returning to the Keys and he to his home in Atlanta. Although they both lived in the southeastern part of the country, a long-distance affair was out of the question. She'd tried it once, only to discover the man had been living a double life with girlfriends on both the east and the west coast.

"I appreciated yesterday and last night, Kim."

She glanced over at him and the corners of her lips eased up. Duan could definitely make her smile, among other things. She considered what he'd just said and wondered how many men actually thanked a woman for sex.

She chuckled. "You're a man who probably appreciates a willing woman. And I was definitely willing." She pushed her plate aside and propped herself against a pillow. "You didn't even have to hit me with any good lines. I saved you the trouble, but it was well worth it."

Over the rim of her coffee cup, she studied him lounging in bed with his robe on. Like her he was naked underneath. He had to be the most sexually compelling man she'd ever met. During their shower they had done a number of scandalous things and she could feel her pulse speed up just thinking about it.

"So tell me something about Duan Jeffries that I may not know," she prompted.

A grin touched his lips. "Is that a prerequisite to sharing a cab ride with you?"

"I could make it one." She smiled. "You never know who you can trust these days."

He laughed. "And you can say that after the past fourteen-plus hours we've shared together?"

"Sure, why not? So tell me."

He took another sip of his coffee. "You tell me what you think you already know."

She scrunched up her face as if she were thinking real hard and Duan couldn't help but chuckle. "Hey, I'm not that complicated."

"Didn't say you were, so let's not get testy," she replied.

She tapped her chin a couple of times. "I know you're thirty-six—used to be a cop and then got promoted to detective. Now you own a P.I. firm with four other guys. You've never been married and as far as anyone knows, you don't have any children. And you date on those rare occasions you're not swarming the country doing investigative work."

"I see my sister's been talking."

Kim shrugged. "What makes you think it was Olivia?"

"Because Terrence knows better. A brother's creed. He won't tell my secrets and I won't tell his."

Kim leaned forward, her brow arched. "Terrence has secrets?"

Amusement flitted in Duan's eyes. "None that Sherri needs to be concerned about, if that's why you're asking. They're all in the past. The Holy Terror is now a changed man."

"So tell me your secrets, Duan. The good, the bad and the ugly."

He smiled. "Um, the good is that I volunteer my time with the boys' club whenever I can." He paused a moment. "The bad is that I have a low tolerance for those who break the law and then, because of some damn loophole in the legal system, get away with it."

Kim heard the anger in his voice. "Is there a particular case that rubbed you the wrong way?"

There was no amusement in his eyes now. "There have been several, but the one that sticks out in my mind is a case I worked involving a woman who was kidnapped, raped and left for dead. We had all the evidence we needed. It should have been open and shut."

"But it wasn't?"

"No. One of our officers obtained evidence without a search warrant."

Kim pulled back, afraid to ask. "They dropped the charges?"

"No, but he was sentenced on a lesser charge."

Kim could understand his frustration. As a nurse she had no tolerance for red tape. She'd seen people who needed to receive treatment denied the care because of administrative issues. That was one of the reasons she transferred to the emergency room. Less red tape.

"More coffee?"

His question pulled her out of her thoughts and she smiled. "No, thanks, I'm good." She stared at him for a moment. "You've told me the good and the bad, so what's the ugly?"

Duan studied his nearly empty cup. Now that was an area he didn't want to cover with her or anyone else. The ugliness in his life was his inability to forgive the person who'd given birth to him. God knew, he'd tried. And he'd gone so far as to search for her as a grown man of thirty, to let her know he'd forgiven her for what she'd done and to find closure for himself.

What he'd found instead was a woman who didn't deserve his forgiveness. Or Terrence's or Libby's. And definitely not the forgiveness of the man who'd loved her.

"That's a discussion for another day," he said, getting off the bed and reaching for the coffeepot. He refilled his cup and glanced over at Kim. "So what about you? What's the good, the bad and the ugly?"

She smiled. "That's easy to answer and I prefer going from last to first."

He tipped his cup at her. "Go ahead."

"The ugly is my father, the wife beater and drunk. I always wanted to become a doctor and he knew it, especially since I was the one who had to heal the bruises Mom got at his hands. For years she worked extra hours to save money to make my dream come true, only for my father to take it out of their bank account when it was time for me to go to college."

She paused a minute. "The bad is that I'll probably never marry because most men see me as too strong-willed. I intimidate the doctors at the hospital, and when it comes to guys outside the hospital, they claim I'm too outspoken. People, mostly men, don't understand me."

Duan figured he must like strong-willed women because he definitely liked her. He would even say he liked outspoken women. And he certainly felt he understood her. She was a woman who didn't mind going after what she wanted. Yesterday, last night and this morning, she had wanted him. He had no complaints.

"What's the good?" he asked.

Her face brightened when she glanced over at the bottle of unopened champagne. "That," she said, pointing to the ice bucket. "I have my own celebrating to do. That's the good."

"What are you celebrating?"

He could swear he saw her chest stick out with pride when she said, "My admission into med school. It took me long enough but I'm going to finally do it."

"Congratulations. What school?" he asked, truly interested.

"University of California, San Francisco." Excitement tinged her voice. "I applied to three others so there's no telling where I might end up if I'm accepted by them, as well. But it doesn't matter really. My dream's finally coming true and I've waited a long time for it."

She was thoughtful a moment. "I'm going to miss being a nurse. I've enjoyed it tremendously, but I feel I have so much more to offer as a doctor."

A huge smile lit his face and he set his cup aside and went back to the bed. Reaching out, he took her hands in his. "I'm happy for you and this does call for a celebration," he said, placing a kiss on her knuckles.

He released her hand and headed for the bucket of champagne. "I usually don't indulge in a drink this early, but it's for a very special occasion." A few moments later he popped the cork and poured some of the bubbly into two flutes.

Kim realized he was genuinely happy for her and it wasn't just a put-on. A conversation she'd once had with Olivia came back to her. His sister told her it had always been Duan's dream to one day own his own P.I. company, but that after college he'd joined the Atlanta police force. However, he'd never lost sight of his dream and a few years ago had started his own P.I. firm.

As Kim watched him cross the room with their champagne, she figured he knew all about following one's dreams. "Thanks," she said, taking the glass he offered.

He smiled down at her and held up his own glass. "I propose a toast to the future Dr. Kimani Cannon."

Kim couldn't help but beam with both pride and excitement as she touched her glass to his and took a sip, enjoying the sparkling taste as it flowed down her throat.

Duan eased on the bed beside her and relieved her of her glass, setting it on the nightstand. "Now for some real celebrating," he said, still holding his glass with one hand while untying the belt at her waist with the other. She wet her lips as she watched him open her robe, revealing her nakedness.

And then with his fingertips he reached up and slowly traced a trail from the base of her throat to her breasts, downward to her navel and lower still to the curls between her thighs.

"So what do you say about us really getting downright festive?" he suggested. And before she figured out what he was about to do, he tilted his glass until champagne splashed on her.

She drew in a sharp breath as the cool liquid contacted her skin. A shiver went through her when it followed the same trail from her breasts downward.

"Oops, sorry, I'm rather clumsy," he said, placing his glass beside hers on the nightstand. "I guess I'm going to have to lick it off you."

And he proceeded to do just that.

KIM'S CELL PHONE RANG the moment she was settled in the backseat of the taxi. She flipped open her phone and smiled after seeing the caller. "Yes, Mom, how are you? You missed a great wedding."

She glanced over at Duan. He was sitting beside her, leaning back against the seat. He had his hand on her thigh and was staring at her with a look that said it wouldn't take much for him to push her down and have his way with her.

She understood. From the moment they'd sneaked out of the wedding reception to make out in that room, something crazy had happened between them. It was like an addiction. One that would hit them with the urge to have sex whenever, wherever and however. The only reason they were controlling themselves now was because they didn't want to scandalize the cab driver. And there was also the risk of getting arrested.

Kim shook her head. This was crazy. Nothing like this had ever happened to her before. It was as if their bodies were acting on impulse without any logical thought. That would explain why two adults had made out in an elevator on the way down to catch their cab.

Sex between them was off the charts, the best she'd ever had. Every orgasm—and there had been plenty— had proven better than the one before. And she appreciated the fact that Duan was such a skillful lover. The past twenty-four hours had been the most pleasure-producing—and memorable—she'd ever had.

"I'm fine, baby, and I hate I missed the wedding," her mother was saying, pulling Kim's attention back to the conversation but not fully away from Duan. She could feel sensations stirring in her belly at his nearness, at the way he was looking at her with all that heat.

"I'll give Sherri a call once she returns from her honeymoon," her mother added. "But now I'm ready to tell you why I wasn't able to join you in Chicago."

"All right." Kim tried to focus completely on the conversation with her mother…at least as much as she could.

Each time she glanced over at Duan she would get aroused. With him she'd gained a boldness that was new to her. To make out with a man in an empty room during her best friend's wedding reception was certainly over the top.

She forced her attention back to her mother. When she had called a few days ago she had been pretty secretive about the reason she could not make the wedding. After convincing Kim that she was fine, Wynona Cannon-Longleaf-Higgins-Gunter had assured her daughter she would tell her everything later.

The last time her mother had behaved in such a manner there had been a man involved. Kim didn't begrudge her mother meeting someone and being happy. At fifty-five Wynona was still attractive, although it had taken Kim a long time to make her mother believe that. Her abusive father had convinced his wife that if she left him, no other man would want her, and where would she be without a man taking care of her.

Unfortunately, Wynona had remained with her husband, taking his abuse, both physically and mentally. Kim would never forget how in her senior year of high school her mother had landed in the emergency room from one of those beatings, and it was then that Wynona had made up her mind it would be the last whipping any man would give her. She had tearfully told Kim she didn't want her daughter to assume that physical abuse was something any woman should tolerate.

While Kim was grateful her mother had finally gotten the strength to leave her dad, the only other thing Wynona needed to rid herself of was the notion that a woman needed a man to survive. That belief was the reason Kim had eventually ended up with three stepfathers. Although none were abusive like her father, the four had lacked substance, and none of the marriages had lasted more than a year or two.

When her mother didn't say anything, Kim prompted, "So, why weren't you able to make it to the wedding, Mom?"

"I've met someone," her mother said.

Kim could hear the excitement in her mother's voice and imagined the giddy smile that must be on her face. *Oh, brother,* she thought, as she leaned back against her seat. The movement brought her closer to Duan and he automatically placed his arm around her shoulder. Heat swept through her as if he'd pressed some button.

"And who did you meet?" Kim heard herself asking her mother.

"His name is Edward Villarosas and he's nice."

They all are in the beginning, Kim thought, remembering the other men her mother had married. First there was Boris Longleaf, whom Wynona had met during her prison ministries. At least he hadn't been a prisoner but one of the guards. He seemed nice enough until her mother had discovered a year into the marriage that Boris preferred men.

Then there was Albert Higgins, a maintenance man in the apartment complex her mother had moved into after her divorce from Boris. There was something about

Albert that Kim hadn't trusted and her suspicions were confirmed when he'd been arrested for his part in a car-theft ring.

And last but not least was Phillip Gunter, the one who'd tried coming on to her. During all her mother's marriages Kim had been away at college and was only around the men whenever she came home for spring break or the holidays.

She'd known from the first moment she'd seen Phillip that he would be trouble, and when he tried cornering her in the laundry room, she had used the knee-jab-in-the-groin move that she'd seen on television. When her mother had rushed downstairs after hearing the man howling in pain, he'd had the audacity to tell her that Kim had been the one trying to come on to him. Of course her mother hadn't believed it and had sent him packing.

So after four failed marriages, Kim hoped her mother would eventually find someone to make her happy. But with Wynona's track record, she wasn't so sure of that happening.

"Tell me all about nice Edward," Kim said, trying to keep the sarcasm out of her voice.

"Edward and I met at the grocery store and things between us began getting serious pretty fast."

Kim rolled her eyes. "I bet."

"You're going to like him."

I doubt it. That's what you said about the others. "When can I meet him?"

"Um, when you come to the wedding in three weeks."

"What!" Kim nearly jumped out of her seat.

"Are you all right, Kim?" Duan asked, leaning close to her in concern. His heated breath against her cheek had sensations stirring within her.

She nodded quickly and whispered, "Yes, I'm fine."

"Kim, who are you with? The man you're engaged to?"

Kim rolled her eyes and shook her head. It had been nearly two months since she'd told that lie and now everyone was still waiting to meet her fiancé.

"Kim?"

Instead of addressing the issue of her fabricated fiancé, she said, "Mom, you can't get married in three weeks. What do you know about this guy?"

"I know enough to believe Edward is a good man. He's a divorcé like me and we enjoy each other's company. He asked me to marry him and I accepted. Be happy for me. I'm happy for you. You don't know how happy I was when you told me and Aunt Gert about your guy. For so long I've blamed myself for you not wanting to get married because I stayed with your father when he was so abusive to me. I know that's what turned you off marriage. I should have left him sooner."

Yes, you should have left him sooner, Kim thought. *Not for my sake but for your own.* Although she would

be the first to admit she'd never wanted to marry because of the abuse she'd witnessed by her father, she
didn't want her mother to feel guilty about that.

Kim pushed frustrated air out of her lungs. "Mom,
please promise you won't do anything until I get there."

"And when do you plan to come? The family wants
me to have another wedding, but Edward and I are tick-
led with the idea of just taking off and flying to Vegas
and—"

"No, Mom, please not Vegas again. Haven't you
learned anything?"

"Kimani Cannon, I won't allow you to take that tone
with me. I didn't call to get your permission to marry
Edward. I'm just letting you know about him. But if you
really want to meet him, then I suggest you make time
to do so."

"I think that I will, Mom."

"Fine. And don't you dare come without bringing
your young man with you," Wynona said in a stern
voice. "I can't wait to meet him, and like I said, the fact
that you're in love has lifted a load off my heart that I've
been carrying around for a long time."

"Mom, I—"

"No, sweetie, please let me finish. I know you don't
understand why I keep going from man to man. Maybe
I'm trying to find something I missed out on all those
years I was with your daddy, letting him hit me around.
I'm fine now. I like Edward. He'll be good for me. But
to know that you've gotten beyond the abuse you saw

in our household has been my prayer. I've been praying for a good man to come into your life and now he has. I can't wait to meet him, so don't you dare think of coming home to Shreveport without him. Goodbye, sweetie."

Her mother hung up and Kim realized she hadn't told her the good news about being accepted into med school. She sighed deeply, knowing she'd gotten herself into a sticky situation with the lie about a fiancé. Sherri had warned her it was bound to catch up with her eventually.

"Is everything all right, Kim?"

Kim glanced over at Duan. For a moment she'd forgotten he was in the taxi with her as they cruised through the streets of Chicago on their way to the airport.

She sighed deeply, and when he opened his arms she cuddled up closer to him. "Is your mother okay?" he asked, concern in his voice.h

Kim chewed on her bottom lip and then said, "If you call planning wedding number five okay, then yes, she's doing just fine."

3

DUAN WASN'T SURE he'd heard her correctly. "Your mother has been married four times?"

"Yes."

He found that simply incredible since his own mother had been married that many times, as well. He shifted in his seat and Kim's body automatically moved with his. He'd done one-night stands before but none had stretched into breakfast the next morning or a cab ride to the airport the next day. When it was over, it was over. There hadn't been any exchange of business cards or promises to follow up. But he knew that he and Kim would see each other again. This weekend hadn't been enough.

"I told you a little about my father being the ugly in my life this morning and how he abused my mother. What I didn't tell you was that they split while I was in high school. I counted it as one of the happiest days of my life. He was a bully of the worse kind."

"And your mom stayed with him all those years?"

"Yes. She was always convinced he would get better. He was smart enough to move us to New Orleans, away from her family during that time. She moved back to Shreveport a few years ago to be close to her family and to take care of my grandmother, who's since died. Now Mom wants to get her life together and believes there is a good man out there destined to be hers. So far she's had four misfits and I'm afraid this fifth might be the same."

He shook his head. It was ironic that her mother was looking for a good man when his mother had had one and hadn't been satisfied. Go figure.

"My mother's been married four times, as well," he heard himself saying.

"She has?"

"Yes." He wondered why he'd told her that. He never discussed his mother with anyone. And it was only on rare occasions that her name came up with Terrence and Olivia.

Kim was sitting close to him, practically in his lap. He felt his desire for her on the rise again and hoped the cab arrived at the airport before he was tempted to do something that could make headlines in the *Chicago Sun-Times*.

"The last I saw her," he said, "she was contemplating husband number five. But that was six years ago. She might have made it to number ten by now."

Kim gave him an odd look. "You're joking, aren't you?"

His expression was unreadable when he said, "I never joke when it comes to the woman who birthed me."

There was an edge of steel in his voice and Kim figured the subject of his mother's desertion was a sore one with him, just like her mother's obsession with finding the perfect man was with her.

The perfect man.

Such a man didn't exist. But that was her mother's dream and Kim knew all about chasing dreams. Just like she understood her mother's desire to see her only child married. Wynona thought she'd failed in both the mother and wife departments. Neither was true, but until mother and daughter were happily married, she would always believe that.

The backseat of the cab got quiet, as if Duan was allowing her time to think, and then he asked, "When is the wedding?"

She rubbed a hand down her face. "They want to marry in three weeks, which will put me in more hot water because of a lie I've told."

"What lie?"

"That I'm engaged."

At his surprised look, she said, "Okay, I'll admit that was a big one, but I had a reason for lying in this case. Mom and her sister, my aunt Gertrude, believe my exposure to my parents' relationship for all those years is the reason I'm not in what they call a *healthy relationship* with a man."

He shrugged. "That's probably true. At least I know it is for me. I'm not sure I can fully trust a woman after what my mother did to my dad. I know all women aren't the same, like I'm sure you know all men aren't the same. But still, it's understandable for anyone who's witnessed all that to want to protect their heart."

Kim nodded. What he said made sense. Her parents' marriage had influenced her way of thinking.

"But I don't want Mom to beat herself up about it and worry unnecessarily. I'm happy with my marital status, and I think Mom would ease off if it wasn't for Aunt Gert. She's a bona fide romantic. She's also a reality TV junkie. A couple of months ago, without me knowing, she submitted my name and bio to *How to Find a Good Man*. Believe it or not, I was the one selected to go on a televised scavenger hunt to find a good man."

Duan chuckled. "You're kidding, right?"

"Trust me, I kid you not. Anyway, they wanted to surprise me, and they sure did when the film crew showed up at the hospital. The only way I could get out of it was to lie and say I'd gotten engaged after Aunt Gert had submitted my personal info."

She shook her head. "That made everyone happy and I was left alone. And to this day, no one has asked me the name of my fiancé. But just like Sherri warned, the lie has caught up with me. Now Mom wants to meet him. I can't put it off any longer."

"Just tell them the truth."

She rolled her eyes. "You don't know my family, especially Aunt Gert. I would go so far as to tell her to butt out of my business, but I know she means well, so I can't. When I go home next week I not only have to meet what could be my fourth stepfather, but also take a man with me to Shreveport as my fiancé. A fake one at least."

Duan thought it might be wise for her to just fess up and tell her family the truth. But if she didn't do that and took a man home…a part of him didn't like the thought of that for some reason. He knew what she did was her business. But still…

"You have any prospects?" he asked, looking down at her. Not for the first time he thought how gorgeous her brown eyes were. He could recall staring into them while climaxing. Several times.

She lifted an arched brow. "Prospects?"

"You know. Guys willing to play the part of your fiancé."

Kim shrugged. She immediately thought of Winslow Breaker. He was a surgeon at the hospital who'd been after her for months. The only problem was that she could just imagine what good old Winslow would expect in return. And she just wasn't feeling it with Winslow. Never had.

"Possibly," she heard herself say.

Duan cursed under his breath, wondering why he even gave a damn. Like he'd thought earlier, what she did was her business.

He noticed the huge marker that indicated the airport was less than ten miles away and knew what he wanted to do before they parted ways.

Shifting in the seat, he reached out and ran the tip of his finger down the side of her face, his gaze fastened on her lips. "Sounds like you have a plan and I'm sure things are going to work out in your favor. In the meantime—" his voice dipped a little lower, became throatier "—I appreciate being with you this weekend."

And then he lowered his mouth to hers.

DUAN HAD THOUGHT her taste was sweet before, but after thrusting his tongue between her parted lips and greedily drinking in her flavor, he realized she was the most alluring woman he'd ever had the pleasure of knowing. Definitely the tastiest.

Their tongues met, melded, mated and were stirring waves of pleasure inside him. And then there was the passion she returned wantonly and flagrantly each and every time they kissed. He would take charge of the kiss, she would follow, and then she would turn the tables and stake her control.

It was while savoring the wet heat and hunger of her sizzling passion that he yielded to full awareness of what being with her entailed. With Kim there was no sensual limit, no restricted areas and no borders to guard. There was just this—absolute surrender and a yearning for more.

"You did say you were flying out on Delta, right, mister?"

Duan released Kim's mouth and inclined his head to look at the taxi driver, who had turned around to stare at them with a silly grin on his face. Understandably so, since he and Kim had been caught in a heated kiss. And he had managed to pull her onto his lap and drape her body across his.

"Yes, I'm flying out on Delta." Then ignoring the man, he leaned up and brushed his lips across hers once more to whisper, "Have a safe trip back to Key West, Kim."

Reluctantly he eased her off his lap. Something pulled inside Duan at the thought that this was where he went his way and she went hers. When the driver brought the taxi to a stop, Duan opened the door and made a move to get out. He then looked back at Kim.

At that moment, something pushed him to say, "I have some free time coming up, so how about adding me to your list of prospects?"

He smiled at the stunned look on her face. "You're serious? You would consider doing that for me?"

"Yes, I would." He reached for her hand, lifted it to his lips and placed a kiss on her knuckles. Immediately he felt the sizzling between them.

Releasing her hand, he shifted and turned to get out of the taxi.

"Don't be surprised if I decide to take you up on your offer, Duan," she warned. "Then all I'll have to concentrate on is making sure Mom knows what she's doing with Edward Villarosas."

Duan turned back, gave her his full attention. Fighting to keep the frown off his face, he repeated, "Edward Villarosas?"

She nodded. "Yes. He's the man my mother plans to marry."

DUAN PULLED OUT his cell phone the moment he cleared security. He wasted no time dialing the number to his office. Landon Chestnut, one of the private investigators who worked with him at the Peachtree Private Investigative Firm, usually came into the office on Sunday afternoons. There were three other guys in the firm—Antron Blair, Brett Newman and Chevis Fleming.

"Hey, man, how was the wedding?" Landon asked, answering on the third ring.

"Real nice. The newlyweds should have reached Paris by now." Duan paused and then asked, "Ready for a blast from the past?"

"About what?"

"It's not what, Landon, but who. Edward Villarosas."

Duan heard his friend's expletives and understood why. Landon had always felt Villarosas was the one he'd let get away when he was still a detective with the force. Duan had already left the department and was working to start his own P.I. business when the Villarosas case had fallen into Landon's lap.

The guy's two wives had come up missing, five years apart, but nothing could be found to connect him with their disappearance. To this day, Duan could recall the frustration and grief Landon had gone through every time he hit a dead end during his investigation. There had been plenty of dead ends but no dead bodies. If Villarosas was guilty, he had covered his tracks well. Landon's failure with the case was one of the reasons he'd left the force to join Duan's P.I. firm.

"I don't think I'll ever forget him," Landon finally said.

"Well, if it's the same Edward Villarosas, and I have a hunch that it is, he's about to remarry," Duan told him, taking a seat near his designated gate.

"Is it to anyone you know?" Landon asked.

"Not directly. The intended bride is the mother of Terrence's wife's best friend. She mentioned it a few moments ago in a cab ride we shared to the airport. Seems he's living in Louisiana now."

"I heard he'd moved from Atlanta. Do you think he told his future bride that on two occasions he was suspected of bumping off his previous wives?"

"I doubt it," Duan said.

"I would have to agree. I'd love to reopen those cases to see if there's anything I missed the first time. The man did have ironclad alibis, but there was something about him that didn't sit well with me. In the end, there was nothing solid that we could use to move the case from missing persons to homicide. He claimed they left him for other men."

"I might have the opportunity to gather more information if I'm invited to the wedding in three weeks. Kimani Cannon needs a date, and I'm figuring since she'll be meeting Villarosas for the first time, she might want to go to Shreveport a little early."

"The opportunity to spend even a week with Villarosas might trip him up to reveal something that he didn't five years ago," Landon said. "During the investigation he had his stories together. Another plus is that he wouldn't recognize you since you had already left the force."

Duan knew Landon was right; he did have an advantage. But he wasn't absolutely certain Kim would ask him to go with her.

"When will you know if you'll be Ms. Cannon's escort?"

"Possibly early next week. I'll give her a call to remind her that I'm available."

"Will you tell her what's going on?"

He considered Landon's question for a moment. If he were to tell Kim, she definitely wouldn't let her mother go through with the wedding. Besides, as much as he might think otherwise, the former cop in him had to remember the man was innocent until proven guilty. And although Villarosas had been a prime suspect in Landon's book, he was never charged with any crime.

"No, I won't tell her yet," he said.

He ended his connection with Landon, and a short while later when the announcer called his flight, he knew that he couldn't waste any time putting a plan into place to make sure he was the man Kim took home to Shreveport with her.

4

KIM WOKE UP MONDAY morning in her own bed with her hormones overacting. And all because of last night's dream, which basically reenacted those moments she'd spent in bed with Duan over the weekend.

There had been something about his touch that was different from any other man's. She chuckled when she recalled Dr. Allen Perry, one of the hospital's prized surgeons, who thought his hands, both in and out of the operating room, were extraordinary. But those hands had nothing on Duan's. The way his fingers had glided across her skin, stroking her in certain areas, especially between her legs, stirring longings in her that she'd never felt before.

She squeezed her eyes shut. Since she was off work today, she could grab another hour or so of sleep, to relive those naughty moments in Duan's arms. She wasn't due back at the hospital until tomorrow, and then she needed to clear her calendar for next week to go home to Shreveport.

She smiled as she remembered growing up in Shreveport among family before her father had convinced her mother to move to New Orleans in search of better job opportunities. That was when the beatings began, and no matter how much Kim had tried, she could not convince her mother to leave him and return home to her family.

The sound of the phone ringing ended any hope of further sleep. Opening her eyes, she leaned up and reached for her cell phone, not recognizing the caller and hoping it was a wrong number. "Hello."

"I'm sitting here at my desk and remembering an incredible weekend."

She smiled, recognizing the deep, husky voice immediately. There was no need to ask how he got her number since she had given it to him before they'd departed the hotel. She'd figured he would look her up the next time he was in the Keys visiting Terrence. She didn't have a problem with him doing that. She had enjoyed his company and his bedroom manners had been perfect.

Kim was also smart enough to know that when a man called to compliment you on how much he enjoyed his time with you, he was probably about to hit you up again for a repeat.

"Can you believe I'm doing the same thing," she said, not feeling the least awkward in admitting it.

"Glad to hear it. And I was wondering…"

A smile of anticipation touched her lips. "Wondering what, Duan?"

"I promised Terrence I'd check on things at his place while he was gone this week. Seems he and Sherri ordered a new bedroom suite and it's to arrive on Friday. I told him I'd be glad to fly to the Keys to make sure it's delivered okay."

A soft chuckle escaped Kim's lips. The new bedroom suite had been Sherri's idea. Her best friend preferred not seeing all those notches on Terrence's bedpost.

"And I was wondering if I could see you again while I'm in town," Duan was saying.

Kim pulled herself up in bed, propped her back against the pillow. There was nothing wrong with enjoying herself as long as she knew what side of the bread was getting buttered. And the one thing she *did* know was that any affair with Duan would be a safe one since he wasn't any more interested in a serious relationship than she was.

Personally, she didn't have the time or inclination for anything serious. Like she'd told Duan, she couldn't fully trust a man because of her dad. And now she had been given the opportunity to pursue the dream that had gotten waylaid for a number of years. She was back on track and there was no man alive who would get her off. Besides, she'd made a decision not to get involved in a long-distance relationship ever again.

And she knew he wasn't interested in anything serious because he'd pretty much made that clear during the cab ride to the airport. He'd stated that he could never fully trust a woman because of his mother.

"I'd love to see you again." And because she knew exactly what this call was about, she added, "To spend time between the sheets with you."

There was no need to be coy, and when it came to sex she had no qualms about taking the driver's seat if she had to, especially if it meant getting where she wanted to go.

There was a slight pause on the line and then he asked, "I love the way you think, Kimani Cannon. How does your schedule look this weekend? Terrence left me the use of his boat and I was thinking about taking it out on Saturday to get in some fishing. Would you like to come along?"

She knew Terrence owned a real forty-foot luxury miniyacht. "Sounds great and I'd love to," she said, thinking of all the possibilities. According to Sherri, Terrence's yacht had a cabin with a comfy bed. Kim doubted they would be doing much fishing, which was fine since she'd never made love on a boat before.

"Wonderful. I'll pick you up at your place Saturday morning around eight. What's the address?"

She rattled it off to him and then they ended the call.

There was no denying it. She was definitely looking forward to this weekend.

DUAN CLICKED OFF the phone and eased back in his chair. He was helpless against the rapid thumping in his chest at the prospect of spending the weekend with Kim again. And deep down he knew that even without the issue of accompanying her to Louisiana, he would still want to spend time with her. The woman had that kind of effect on him, something he still didn't quite understand.

He'd had sexual encounters of the most intense kind before, but what he'd shared this past weekend with Kim had been so incredible that even now he could barely breathe just thinking about it.

There was nothing like waking up to a hot feminine body next to his, an early morning hard-on poking between a pair of curvaceous buttocks.

His mouth had traveled every inch of her and he remembered how she would shiver with awareness all the way to her toes when he licked certain parts of her. He didn't know of a more responsive woman.

But a part of him knew it had been more than just the sex. He'd enjoyed talking to her, and because she'd had issues with one of her parents while growing up, she'd known exactly how he felt regarding his mother.

He glanced up at the knock on his door and wasn't surprised when the four men walked in. Landon Chestnut. Chevis Fleming. Brett Newman. Antron Blair. Due to the number of cases they handled and the traveling involved, it was unusual for all five of them to be in the same place at the same time.

Duan had met the four while working as a cop in Atlanta. They had started the academy together and had eventually gotten promoted to detectives. He had been the first to venture out on his own and Landon followed. Within another year, Brett and Chevis had joined them as partners.

Antron had eventually followed in his father's footsteps and become an FBI agent until an undercover sting operation had nearly ended his life. After that, he'd decided to join the others at the firm.

What Duan liked about their setup was that, although they worked individual cases, each had a specialty. He had an analytical mind and was good at deciphering leads from an investigative report. Landon had a knack for finding missing persons. Chevis had a gift when it came to interrogations. Brett was computer savvy and was considered their technical expert, and Antron had exemplary undercover skills, and his contacts within the FBI were invaluable.

Over the past five years they had handled a number of cases, working closely with their allies in the Atlanta police department and the attorney friends they'd met over the years.

"Landon told us you might be working on a case and you could use our help," Brett said.

"Yes." Duan nodded. "It would definitely make things a lot easier. I know you have your own cases, but I'd appreciate your assistance in checking into a few things."

It didn't take long for him to provide the details. First they would contact a detective they knew with the Atlanta police department to reopen the two cases. Then they would gather information to see what Villarosas had been up to since he'd moved from Atlanta a few years ago. They also needed to contact the family and any friends of the missing women to see if either woman had been sighted or heard from since her disappearance. There was still the chance the women *had* run off with other men like Villarosas claimed. However, for two wives to do the same thing was a bit of a stretch.

After the guys had left his office, Duan settled back in his chair once again. He was determined that before Kim's mother married Edward Villarosas, they would know whether he was guilty of killing his former wives.

5

LIKE CLOCKWORK KIM's doorbell rang at eight o'clock on Saturday morning. She glanced down at herself as she headed for the door. The weather forecast indicated it would be a beautiful day for boating and she was wearing a new outfit for the occasion.

She opened the door and a blade of sunlight came through, nearly blinding her, but not before she took stock of the man standing on her doorstep. She angled her head and squinted to look up at him. He flashed a sexy smile and immediately she felt weak in the knees. It was going to be one of those days when she would find it almost impossible to keep her hands off him. He had just that kind of an effect on women. Her in particular. Standing there in a pair of jeans that tapered down muscular thighs, a T-shirt covering his broad shoulders, he looked every bit of sexy and that wasn't helping matters any. For a split second, all she could do was stand there and drool.

"Good morning, Kim."

It took her a moment to find her voice and respond. But watching the movement of his mouth had made her remember all the things that same mouth had done to her. Naughty, naughty. "Good morning, Duan."

"Are you ready?"

A memory of being ready for him—naked and waiting—flickered through her mind and she forced it away. "Yes, I just need to grab my jacket and bag."

"All right. Take your time."

Kim quickly headed back into her living room to collect the jacket and duffel bag. She knew the moment Duan stepped over the threshold to enter her home and closed the door. The air between them began to thicken and it seemed as if the air-conditioning had stopped working. Heat was coming through the vents instead.

He gave her living room an appreciative glance before turning his dark eyes to her. Every nerve in her body felt stretched tight when his gaze roamed over her, as if he could see through her outfit. He'd seen her naked before, had tasted practically every inch of her skin, and he knew all her hot spots and exactly what he needed to do to make them hotter.

She swallowed, wondering if he was thinking about any of those things. Was he remembering last weekend like she was doing? Was he as aware of her as she was of him? From the way his eyes were darkening, she figured he was.

"I guess it's not going to happen, Kim," he said, breaking the silence, his husky voice making her nipples harden.

She pulled in a deep breath. "What's not going to happen?"

"That we can wait to get to the boat before we do anything."

She could really play dumb and ask what he meant, but figured why waste her time or his. Goose bumps formed on her skin and she couldn't help skimming her gaze over him like he'd done with her earlier. She had already checked him out pretty good at the front door. But now, thanks to the huge bulge behind his zipper, there was more of him, and the woman in her appreciated that fact.

"So what do you think we need to do about it?" he asked.

"Why think?" In addition to the thrumming sensations in the pit of her stomach, she could also feel the steam floating between them.

He was right. They couldn't wait. Their desire for each other was urgent. It was spontaneous. And like before, they needed to deal with it right now. She didn't have a problem with that and proceeded to yank her T-shirt over her head, glad she wasn't wearing a bra.

Duan didn't waste any time crossing the room and pulling Kim into his arms. And when she parted her lips, he thrust his tongue between them until it was firmly planted inside her mouth. His hands were on the move and the moment his fingers found her breasts, his erection strained against his zipper. Touching her nipples wasn't enough. He needed to taste them. He remembered her flavor well and intended to become reacquainted with it this weekend.

His mouth replaced his fingers as he ended the kiss, drawing her nipples between his lips and sucking hard. He heard her moan deep in her throat, and when she clutched his head to hold it to her breasts, his hands automatically lowered and slid between the waistband of her shorts.

Shit. She's not wearing panties, either.

His erection became even more engorged when he touched bare skin, then delved into the thickness of the curls covering her sex. The moment his hand touched her intimately, her thighs automatically parted and he eased his fingers into her soft flesh, the essence of her dewy core. He pushed apart her legs even more with his knee, and still latching on to her breasts with his mouth, he inserted his fingers deeper inside her. The moment he found her clit, she exploded in a climax of gigantic proportions and he clamped his mouth on hers to smother her scream.

The scent of her orgasm filled the air and he pulled the aroma deep into his nostrils. Before she could recover, he swept her into his arms and carried her over to the kitchen table and placed her on top of it.

His hands grasped the waistband of her shorts and pulled them down her legs. Before she could open her eyes, he lowered his head between her thighs, hungry enough to eat her alive.

His teeth scraped across her clit then he eased the torture with the tip of his tongue as he tasted her deeply.

He couldn't remember the last time he'd taken a woman on her kitchen table and quickly realized he'd never done such a thing. It seemed everything with Kim was wild, spontaneous and crazy. And when he felt her on the brink of yet another orgasm, he didn't intend to let her have it without him.

He pulled away and, still feasting his gaze on her body stretched out before him, kicked off his shoes and proceeded to remove his clothes. Standing in her kitchen completely naked, he put on a condom and turned his full attention back to her.

Duan reached out and wrapped her legs around his neck. Then he parted her thighs and entered her, going all the way to the hilt. He tried to maintain control of his senses but her body seemed to be summoning him on a primal level and he was too weak to deny the call. Not that he intended to.

Mercy. The feel of being back inside her was sending all kinds of sensations rippling through him. Grabbing firmly on to her thighs, he began thrusting inside her while her body rocked with every movement he made. He knew the exact moment he'd touched her G-spot and the stroking took on a whole new meaning.

He watched her expression each time he entered and withdrew, keeping up the rhythmic pace while her inner muscles clenched him tight, trying to milk him for all they could get. He'd never made love before with this intensity, this need. This hunger. He couldn't explain it. Wouldn't know how to explain it. Right now he could only accept it. This fiery mating. One that touched every fiber of his being. Every part of his soul.

And then he felt her shudder, felt the way she arched her back, the way her legs tightened around his neck, and knew he had to push both of them over the edge.

He thrust harder and the sound of her scream made something inside him snap. He needed this mating like he needed his next breath and he lifted her hips in his hands for a deeper penetration. Head flung back, his body bucked into yet another explosion without fully recovering from the first.

He kept going until there was nothing left inside him. After giving it all, he slumped down on her and took a quick lick of her breasts before his face settled blissfully between them.

IT WAS A BEAUTIFUL DAY to be out on the ocean and to Duan's surprise the fish were biting. He enjoyed fishing and recalled it was one of the few things he and Terrence did with their father that didn't include Olivia. It wasn't that she hadn't been invited to go with them, but after he'd shown her how to bait her hook that first time, she had refused to come back.

He glanced over at Kim. She looked beautiful sitting on the bench seat next to him in one hot-looking bikini, the sunlight dancing off her features. She claimed this was her first time fishing, and she hadn't been at all squeamish when he'd shown her how to bait the hook. She reminded him that she was a nurse and nurses didn't get woozy at the sight of blood and guts.

She had been thrilled at her first catch and a part of him was excited about having her there. He'd gotten used to fishing alone, preferring the solitude. But not today. He wasn't ready to figure out why.

Another thing he had to get his mind around was the intense chemistry between them. The sexual chemistry was so strong, so overwhelming, that the need to have each other took precedence over anything else. Sounded crazy, but it was true.

Prime example was the incident back at her place. He had taken her on her kitchen table, of all places. His only excuse was that he'd arrived this morning filled with one hell of a lustful need after thinking about her, dreaming of her, all week.

The moment she'd opened the door, every primitive male instinct within him had erupted. He figured no woman had a right to look so damn good that early. He wasn't even sure whether she was wearing makeup. Didn't matter. And she had a baseball cap on her head. That didn't matter either. What mattered was that she was a woman his body seemed to desire whenever he saw her. Any time and any place.

She was becoming an addiction.

She must have felt his gaze and looked up from working her fishing pole. "I like doing this, Duan."

He chuckled as he leaned back in his seat and tilted his cap back. It was on the tip of his tongue to say he liked doing her. "It's hard to believe you've lived in the Keys for over a year now and have never gone fishing. What a waste of water." He noticed the hands holding the fishing rod. Most women he dated did up their nails but not Kim. He figured in her line of work it was best she didn't. He liked her fingers. He remembered sucking on them the last time. The memory made something pull deep within his groin.

"Well, to be honest, I'm not much for being out on or in the water," she said, interrupting his thoughts. "Makes me nervous."

He lifted his brow. "Then how did you learn to swim?"

"I didn't."

He stared at her, not believing what she'd said. "You don't know how to swim?"

"No. I always planned to take lessons but ended up chickening out."

He glanced around and then back at her. "So, you're out here with me in the middle of the ocean, wearing a very sexy bathing suit, and don't know how to swim."

She smiled. "The key words are that I'm out here with you. You won't let anything happen to me. Sherri will never forgive you if you do."

He returned her smile. He could believe that. "I've never asked how the two of you met."

She leaned back and propped her feet up on the side of the boat. He liked the way her bathing suit fit. She had used the facilities below to change out of the shorts set into the bikini as soon as they'd gotten on the boat. He had changed into swimming trunks, as well. It was a beautiful day in April and there were other boaters taking advantage of the perfect weather.

"Sherri and I met in college and were roommates for all four years. After college we decided to pursue opportunities in the same cities. If it wasn't for Sherri, I would probably still be living in D.C. She talked me into moving to the Keys. My life hasn't been the same since."

He nodded. "Is that good or bad?"

"At the time it was good because I needed a change. The guy I was involved with wanted more out of the relationship than I was willing to give. He knew going in that I wasn't looking for anything long-term and claimed he wasn't, either. Somewhere along the way he changed his mind."

"But he didn't change yours."

It was presented as a statement and not a question, but she answered anyway. "I doubt there is anything or anyone that will change my mind about that."

She paused for a moment. "I told you about my father and all his ugliness. Well, then there was that one time one of my stepfathers tried to come on to me. If I hadn't known a little about defending myself, there's no telling what might have happened. His actions only added to my distrust of men in general."

The thought of someone trying to take advantage of her filled him with anger. "So there's never been anyone you'd want to marry?"

A bright smile touched her lips. "Sure," she joked. "Denzel Washington. But I don't see Pauletta giving him up anytime soon. But on a serious note, I've told you my reasons for not wanting to indulge in a long-term affair. Short-term serves me just fine. I watch my mother live her life believing she can't survive without a man and I refuse to let that happen to me, so marriage is not in my future."

He knew the feeling.

"But I do like kids and want to have a child someday," she added.

Her statement didn't surprise him. Although he'd never seen her around children, for some reason he believed she would be a good mother and nothing like the woman who'd birthed him. As far as kids went for him, he liked them but wasn't sure he could ever be the father his dad had been. Orin Jeffries had been a rock for his kids. He had always been there for them, and when his poor excuse of a wife had walked out, he had taken on the role of single father without much sweat.

Duan pulled in a deep breath, wondering who he was fooling. He shifted his gaze from Kim and stared out over the water, thinking that for his father, there had been *both* sweat and tears. He would never forget the day he'd walked in on his father standing in the middle of his bedroom, staring at his wife's picture and crying. Actually crying over the woman who'd humiliated him by running off with another man. Duan had backed out of the room without his father knowing he'd been there. That day stuck out in his mind because it was then that he'd decided he didn't want any woman to ever cause him the pain he'd seen on his father's face.

"What about you?" Kim asked.

He glanced back over at her. "What about me?"

"How do you feel about marriage and children?"

It had been a long time since any woman asked him that. "I don't ever plan to marry. And as long as there are such things as condoms, I don't ever intend to produce a baby, either, although I like them. I just don't want to parent one. Don't know how good I'd be, so I'd rather not take any chances." He turned from Kim and stared out over the ocean again.

"I guess we'll have to wait on Sherri and Terrence."

He glanced back at her. "Wait on them for what?"

She smiled. "Babies. I'll be godmother to any baby they have. That's a given."

He couldn't help but chuckle at that. "Is it?"

"Yes."

And any baby his brother and sister-in-law produced would make him an uncle. *Uncle Duan.* He liked the sound of that, but he wasn't so sure it would be Terrence and Sherri who would be bestowing the honor upon him first. For some reason, he had a feeling it would be Reggie and Libby.

Deciding to change the subject to the one they needed to discuss, he asked, "How are things with your mother?"

The face she made told him the answer before she opened her mouth to say anything. "Basically the same. I've talked to her twice this week and at least she's agreed not to do anything rash about her marital status until after I get there."

"When are you leaving?"

"Friday, and I plan to be there for a week. That will give me a few days to spend with her and to get to know the man she wants to marry."

He nodded. "And are you still contemplating taking a fake fiancé with you?"

She tilted her head back and met his gaze. "It depends."

He lifted a brow. "On what?"

"On whether or not you were serious about going with me."

THERE, SHE'D SAID IT and now she was trying to decipher his response, Kim thought, studying Duan. She had been tempted to bring up the subject all morning but hadn't known how to.

Although he'd made the offer last weekend, it had been post-sex, when they'd still been caught up in the hot time they'd shared in her hotel room. When she'd played the offer over and over in her mind this week, she'd tried to convince herself that he had been serious, but she wasn't so sure. This was one way to find out for certain.

He placed his fishing pole aside and leaned over her. "Then I guess I just became your pretend fiancé since I was dead serious, Kim."

She swallowed. He was giving her *that* look. "You do know what that will mean when it comes to my mother and aunt, don't you? They will be asking you questions, trying to pin us down to a wedding date and all that stuff. It won't be easy."

He shrugged. "And it won't be hard. You tell me what to say and I'll say it."

She tilted her head and continued to hold his gaze. "And just what will you get out of this?"

A smile touched his lips and that smile made sensations flutter all through her. "I'm surprised that you would ask me that, especially after last weekend and this morning," he said in a throaty voice. "But just in case you don't have a clue, let me break it down to you." He leaned closer. "I'll be getting you, Kimani. I like kissing you. I enjoy having sex with you."

His smile widened as he added, "Um, I *especially* like having sex with you."

She couldn't help noticing he'd specifically pointed out they'd had sex and not made love. Why did his description of what they'd done bother her, when the same terminology from any other man would not have? She pushed the thought from her mind and wriggled up to wrap her arms around his neck. Looking up at him, she smiled. "Then I guess we are officially pretend engaged."

"DUAN ACTUALLY VOLUNTEERED to go to Shreveport and pretend to be your fiancé?" Sherri asked Kim a few days later. Terrence had left their hotel room to grab them breakfast and she'd taken the time to give Kim a call.

"Yes, can you believe my luck? Seeing me with him will satisfy Aunt Gert I've got a man."

"Is there something you aren't telling me about you and Duan, Kim? Sounds serious."

Kim chuckled. She knew just what Sherri was hinting at. "Not serious, just sexual. I don't do serious, Sherri. You of all people know that. And Duan isn't looking for anything serious, either. It's the perfect arrangement."

Before her best friend could ask her any more questions, Kim quickly said, "Now hang up the phone before your husband returns. You *are* on your honeymoon, you know."

"I know, and I am so happy I have to pinch myself to make sure it's real."

Kim could hear the sheer contentment in Sherri's voice. She laughed. "Why pinch yourself? Just look at the size of that rock on your hand if you have any doubt."

Moments later, she hung up the phone and glanced across the room at her packed luggage. She would be flying out of the Keys in a few hours and would catch a connecting flight in Atlanta, where Duan would be joining her to continue on to Shreveport.

Strolling from the living room to the kitchen, she couldn't help but smile when she glanced over at her table. She was consumed with memories every time she walked past it. Even now her mind was filled with memories of their lovemaking on Terrence's boat. To be totally honest, there wasn't a single night since the wedding that she hadn't thought about all the lovemaking she and Duan had done.

He was definitely a man who knew how to have a good time and she remembered how quickly she had slid her bikini bottoms down her legs and untied her top. It hadn't taken Duan any time at all to remove his swimming trunks, and using the rocking motion of the boat on the water, they had taken each other hard, fast and often.

And they would be back together again for a third weekend. She shouldn't, but she was beginning to consider him as her weekend lover, and his ability to turn any fantasy she'd ever had into reality was simply amazing.

Kim glanced at her watch. It was time to begin loading her luggage in the car. As she headed up the stairs she couldn't squash her anticipation at the thought that in a few hours she would be seeing Duan again.

6

DUAN PULLED INTO the airport parking lot and then into the space his car would occupy for the next ten days. He patted the pocket of his shirt to make sure the ring he'd slid inside was still there. He had volunteered to come up with an engagement ring and thought the one he already had in his possession was perfect. It was the ring his grandmother had left him to present to the woman he would one day marry. When he'd mentioned it to Kim, she'd thought using that ring was a good idea, as well.

He had to remind himself that the ring's purpose was twofold. First, it was personal since he was helping out a woman he'd come to consider a friend. It was also business, in that he hoped to determine if Edward Villarosas was guilty of murder.

The Atlanta police department had agreed to reopen the two cases and was putting together a list of family and friends that would be interviewed again. According to the cold case file, wife number one hadn't returned home from what should have been a weekend trip to Orlando with her two girlfriends ten years ago.

The other women acknowledged that Mandy Villarosas had been acting strange and had left their hotel room right after breakfast, saying she was meeting someone. When she hadn't returned for lunch, they'd begun to worry and had called Edward, who'd encouraged them to notify the police.

The other women claimed they had no idea who Mandy was supposed to meet, but indicated there had been a man in a club the night before who Mandy had been flirting with. Two years later, Villarosas had divorced his wife on grounds of desertion, and a year after that, he remarried.

He and Sandra Villarosas had been married two years when he'd reported her missing. She hadn't shown up for work and one of her coworkers had gotten concerned. Edward was out of town on a fishing trip in Florida with friends and had left two days before. In fact, Sandra was the one who had taken him to the airport. Several witnesses verified that, and also the fact she had been seen around town afterward.

Neither woman had been heard from since, and Edward's alibis were verified by family and friends.

Duan walked inside the airport terminal, which was busy as usual. Any other day he might have wished he were someplace else, even in his office totally absorbed in another case. But not today.

If Kim's flight left on time she would be here in less than an hour. It had been five days since they'd been together and he was anxious to see her again. With that admission, he felt a punch to his stomach and something close to panic. He was reminded that the last thing he needed to do was get wrapped up with any woman. Women, he knew for a fact, had the ability to wrap a man around their finger, then walk away and not look back.

Instead he switched his thoughts from Kim to the real purpose of this trip. Edward Villarosas. Going to Shreveport to meet Kim's family would afford him the opportunity of being in the man's company for almost a week, and with a bit of luck he'd notice or discover something that the other detectives who'd worked the case hadn't. For the time being, the less Kim knew about what was going on, the better.

If Villarosas was guilty, then he was a man who'd successfully gotten away with two crimes. It was going to be up to Duan to figure out how Kim's mother played into any of this. Was the man looking to knock off wife number three? He had read the two case files over and over, and there was nothing in them to indicate Villarosas was a man who married women and then got some sort of sick kick getting rid of them.

But Duan did not intend on taking any chances. He would be on full alert until he figured out just what type of man they were dealing with. At no time did he plan on putting Kim or her mother in danger. A deep frown settled on his face at the thought of anything happening to Kim. He would protect her with his life if he had to, and wouldn't let Villarosas or anyone else harm a single strand of hair on her head or her mother's.

Right now he didn't want to question why he'd become so protective of Kimani; he just accepted that was the way it was. While his partners were out in the field gathering information, Duan's job in Shreveport over the next few days was to get close to Villarosas and develop a rapport with him in hopes the man would let his guard down.

Even without meeting the guy he had a gut feeling the man was bad news, and the quicker that could be proven, the better.

Kim glanced around when she approached her gate. Duan's head could be seen above everyone else's, making him easily recognizable. In addition to that, he was the man most women were giving a second look.

She glared at one such woman when she passed, then frowned, wondering why it annoyed her that other women found him as desirable as she did. It wasn't like he was her man. Everything between them was strictly casual. They enjoyed having sex with each other. No big deal.

Kim breathed in deeply, wondering who she was fooling. It was beginning to become a big deal. There was something about this affair with Duan that was different. Emotions were starting to come into play, at least on her end, and she never let emotions creep into any of her relationships. There was no place for them.

And as she got closer to where he stood, she didn't want to analyze what those strange feelings were about. The only thing she wanted to do was concentrate on him. He was wearing a polo shirt and a pair of khaki pants and he looked good. Instinctively, she walked into his open arms and a part of her wished all those drooling women took notice.

"Good seeing you again, Kim," he murmured, brushing a kiss across her temple.

The moment his lips touched her skin, Kim felt the muscles in her belly tighten. He pulled her closer and she melted into him easily. Already he was hard and erect. She tilted her head and looked up at him. There was never any other way with them. Their desire for each other was spontaneous. They saw; they wanted.

"That was just a public kiss," he whispered. "I'm going to give you a very private one later when we're alone."

She smiled. "I can't wait. And speaking of waiting, have you been here long?"

He shrugged as he released her and took her hand. "This is a busy airport so I figured it was best to arrive early. There are a couple of eating places around here if you're hungry. We have a couple of hours before our flight leaves."

"No, I'm fine. What about you?"

That elicited a laugh. "I could use something else but will settle for a cup of coffee."

She had an idea what he meant. "Okay."

He took her hand and led her toward the food court. He glanced over at her. "You look cute."

"Thanks."

She had deliberately worn this outfit, a short denim skirt and a green tank top with spaghetti straps. She hadn't missed the way he'd scanned her appreciatively from head to toe.

She followed him to an empty table and a waitress came to take Duan's coffee order. Before the woman left he glanced over at her. "You sure you don't want anything?"

"Um, I would like some vanilla ice cream."

He lifted a brow after the waitress walked off. "Ice cream? This early?"

She laughed. "It's not *that* early, Duan." She checked her watch. "In fact, it's a few minutes past ten. I love ice cream and I'm known to eat it for breakfast. It used to drive Sherri crazy."

He smiled. "I bet. And before I forget, give me your left hand."

Instinctively she did as he asked and watched him pull a small jewelry box out of his shirt pocket. He placed it on the table beside her and opened it up.

"Wow! It's beautiful, Duan." And she meant it. The ring was dazzling. "And this was your grandmother's?"

"Yes," he said, taking it out of the box and sliding it onto her ring finger. It was a perfect fit and she watched in surprise as he lifted her hands and kissed her knuckles.

"When she died she left it for me since I was her oldest grandson," he said, releasing her. "However, since I have no plan to ever marry I thought about giving it to Terrence, but Dad figured I should keep it anyway since it was left to me. I think she felt bad for the way her daughter turned out."

Kim fluttered her fingers, admiring the ring Duan had just placed on it. "Well, regardless, I think it's beautiful and—"

"Oh, my goodness! Did the two of you just get engaged?"

Both Kim and Duan glanced up at their waitress. She was standing there holding a coffee in one hand and a cup of vanilla ice cream in the other, a delighted look on her face.

Kim opened her mouth to answer but Duan beat her to the punch. "Yes, we did."

"Congratulations!" the woman exclaimed. "That's wonderful and it's a beautiful ring."

A huge smile spread over Duan's face. "Thanks."

He glanced expectantly at Kim. She then caught on to what he was doing and smiled up at the woman. "Yes. Thanks."

The waitress placed the coffee in front of Duan and gave Kim her ice cream. She gave both of them another huge smile before leaving. Kim leaned over the table. "Why did you let her think we've just gotten engaged?"

He shrugged. "For all intents and purposes, we have."

She rolled her eyes. "We're role-playing for Mom and Aunt Gert, not necessarily for strangers."

He chuckled. "Who's to say she doesn't know someone who might know you? You'd be surprised how small this world is sometimes. Besides, telling her we're engaged gave me some practice time."

"Practice for what?"

"Smiling whenever anyone congratulates us. I'm sure we'll be hearing a lot of that over the next few days. Did I seem genuinely pleased?"

She momentarily clamped her mouth shut, not sure what to say or to question why she felt irked by what he'd said. Of course they were role-playing, but for some reason she was bothered by the thought.

When he continued to stare at her, waiting for her response, she pasted a smile on her face and said in a syrupy tone, "You were simply marvelous, darling."

He wiggled his eyebrows. "Ready for an Oscar?"

She rolled her eyes. "Um, I wouldn't go that far."

He laughed as he reached out and took her hand in his, caressing the finger that wore his ring. "But you would say I was good, wouldn't you?"

The smile that touched her lips that moment was genuine. "Yes, Duan, you were good."

And then she gently pulled her hand away from his to eat her ice cream.

7

"Duan, I'd like you to meet my mother, Wynona Cannon-Longleaf-Higgins-Gunter. Mom, this is Duan Jeffries, my fiancé."

Duan kept his mouth from dropping completely open. Kim's mother was a very attractive woman. Kim had said she was fifty-five, but to his way of thinking, she looked a lot younger. He offered the older woman his hand. "How do you do, Mrs...." Already he'd forgotten her names.

She beamed happily. "Just call me Wynona. I don't know why Kim insisted on saying all those names."

Kim smiled. "Because they're yours. All four of them." She glanced around. "And where is the man who might be number five?"

Wynona gave her daughter a frown. "Edward will be here any minute. He's probably stuck in traffic since he lives on the other side of town."

She returned her attention to Duan. "Your last name is Jeffries?"

"Yes, ma'am."

"And before you ask, Mom, the answer is yes," Kim said. "He's Terrence's older brother."

"Best friends marrying brothers. How nice."

She studied his features for a moment and then asked, "And you're willing to wait for Kim to finish med school before the two of you marry?"

Duan gave Kim a loving smile and slipped his arm around her waist to bring her closer. That was number one on the list of questions Kim had known her mother would ask. Wynona had asked her that same thing when she'd told her mother about her acceptance into medical school. Evidently she was hoping for a different answer.

"Whatever Kim wants, that's what we'll do," he said, leaning over and placing a kiss on Kim's lips. He could tell from the expression that appeared on Wynona's face that she wasn't pleased with his comment.

"But we're talking about four, maybe five years," the older woman pointed out. "Don't you think that's way too long to wait?"

He opened his mouth to respond but Kim beat him to it. "Maybe you ought to try it, Mom. You, of all people, should know that rushing into marriage serves no purpose other than a quick divorce. Which is why I think you and Mr. Villarosas should take more time to get to know each other before the two of you contemplate marriage."

Instead of agreeing or disagreeing with Kim's comment, Wynona smiled at him and said, "And what do you do for a living, Duan?"

"I used to be a cop but now I'm a private investigator. I own my own business." Now he knew how it felt to be interrogated.

"And I take it that you love my daughter."

Duan looked at Kim again, and something about being asked that question bothered him. Nonetheless, he plastered a smile on his face before saying, "Very much so. I wouldn't be marrying her if I didn't."

Wynona opened her mouth, but at that moment there was a knock at the door. She smiled. "Excuse me. That's probably Edward."

As soon as Wynona exited the room Kim turned to Duan. "So far so good. You're handling Mom's interrogation well."

Before Kim could say anything else, Wynona returned with a tall, slender man by her side. He was smiling as he approached them.

"Well, now, Wynona, this has to be your daughter. She favors you." He came to stand before Kim and Duan, but only gave Duan a cursory glance. Kim had his full attention.

"Yes, Edward, this is my daughter," Wynona said, beaming proudly. "Kim, this is the man I plan to marry in a few weeks."

Kim extended her hand to him. "Nice meeting you, Edward. And this is the man I plan to marry, Duan Jeffries. Duan, this is Edward Villarosas."

It was only then that Edward met Duan's gaze, and Duan felt the smile he bestowed upon him wasn't genuine. That feeling in his gut intensified. "Duan, nice meeting you." Edward offered him his hand.

"Likewise," Duan said, taking it.

Wynona leaned close to Edward. "Don't they make a lovely couple, Edward?"

Edward smiled up at her. "Just as lovely as we do." He then turned his attention back to Kim. "I understand you have doubts about me making your mother happy."

Kim lifted a brow. "And you plan to rid me of those doubts, right?"

He chuckled. "I certainly do. Your mother is the only woman for me."

"So this is your first marriage?" Duan asked, pinning the man with a direct gaze.

Villarosas seemed surprised by the question, and the look he gave Duan indicated he didn't appreciate being asked. "No. In fact I've been married twice and both ended in divorce."

Duan nodded. At least Villarosas was up front about that.

"But I'm determined to make sure this time is the last time," he added, taking Wynona's hand to his lips and kissing her knuckles.

A part of Duan wished everything the man said was true. That he was innocent in the disappearances of his two wives. Not for Villarosas's sake but for Kim's mother's sake. She was a nice lady who deserved better.

"Mom, Duan and I are going to check in to the hotel now and—"

"But Gert will want to come by later to see you," Wynona said.

Kim shrugged. "I'll see Aunt Gert tomorrow. We'll come join you and her for breakfast since I know you're making a big deal out of it in the morning. I can just imagine who all you've invited."

Wynona smiled. "Just family and friends. They're looking forward to seeing you and meeting Duan."

Kim chuckled. "I just bet they are, but I had a rough week at work and the flight was a long one and I want to rest up a bit. So, we'll see you in the morning." Turning to Edward, she said, "It was nice meeting you, Edward."

"Same here, Kim." He glanced over at Duan. "And you, too."

Duan almost laughed at that. "Likewise, Edward," he said with a serious expression.

Duan and Kim were about to walk out the door when Edward called out, "Sorry, Duan, but you didn't say what you did for a living."

Duan wondered what business it was of Villarosas's, but answered, "Yes, I did, but you weren't here at the time. I'm an ex-cop turned private investigator."

Villarosas's brows lifted. "In Key West?"

Duan smiled. "No, in Atlanta."

Villarosas wasn't quick enough to hide the startled look in his eyes. And Duan could just imagine the questions rolling around in the man's mind right about now.

"And you didn't say what you did for a living, Edward," Duan ventured.

Again Villarosas seemed taken aback that Duan would question him about anything. He hesitated a moment before saying, "I'm retired."

"Oh, I see." Duan placed his hand in the center of Kim's back and they continued out the door.

KIM WALKED INTO THE hotel room and tossed her purse on the sofa. She wished she could read Duan's thoughts. He had been quiet during most of the car ride from her mother's and she wanted to know what he was thinking.

She doubted it was obvious to her mother, whose inability to read people was legendary, but it hadn't gone unnoticed by her that Duan had taken an immediate dislike to Edward and she wondered why.

She glanced over at Duan and noticed him looking around the room. After they had picked up a rental car, they had come here directly from the airport but only long enough to drop off their luggage before heading over to her mother's place. Now they were back and he was checking things out.

The suite had a separate sitting room with a sofa that pulled out to a bed. There was a spacious bath with a hot tub and the bedroom area had a king-size bed. There was no doubt in her mind that she and Duan would be sharing that bed.

"I have an idea what you're thinking, Duan," she said.

It was then that he glanced over at her. "I doubt very seriously that you do. But if you want to take a stab at it, then go ahead and tell me."

"You're probably wondering what the hell you're doing here, and wishing you were someplace else."

He looked down at the carpeted floor and then lifted his gaze back to hers. "I'm alone in this hotel room with you, with a king-size bed, and you think I'd rather be someplace else?"

She released an exasperated laugh. "Be serious, Duan."

He stared at her for a moment. "I am serious when it comes to you, me and the bed."

She nodded. "And how serious are you about Edward? I could tell you don't like him. Why?"

Duan moved across the room to stand in front of Kim. She had asked a good question, and maybe it would be best for all concerned if he answered it. To be fair to the man, he hadn't planned to tell her what he suspected until he had something concrete, not speculation. But Kim was very observant, and it would be best for the investigation if he leveled with her now and hoped she would understand and not blow his cover.

"Duan?"

"We need to talk." He reached out and took her hand in his and gently led her toward the couch. She sat beside him and he saw the curiosity in her eyes.

Her hand tightened on his. "What is it, Duan?"

He muttered a silent curse. He would tell her, but he would also make sure she understood that although Villarosas might think Duan was onto him, it was important to keep him guessing. Duan had long ago discovered that a man with something to hide would begin messing up if he thought he had a reason to look over his shoulder.

He pulled in a deep breath and began talking. "The moment you mentioned Edward Villarosas's name to me that day we were leaving Chicago, it sounded familiar. All it took was a phone call to one of my partners for confirmation."

Kim's eyes widened. "Your partner? Are you saying Edward is in some kind of trouble?"

"I'm not sure yet."

Kim shook her head and released Duan's hand to stand. She stared down at him with numerous questions in her eyes. "Not sure? Duan, we're talking about a man my mother is planning to marry. Just what *are* you sure about?"

Duan stood also. He knew she was not going to like what he was about to tell her, and would probably wonder why he hadn't told her sooner. "A few years ago, on two occasions, Edward came under suspicion for a crime, but nothing was proven."

Kim placed her hands on her hips and met his gaze. Duan could clearly see the worried look in her eyes. "What was he suspected of doing?"

A part of Duan wished they weren't having this conversation, but another part of him was glad they were. He hadn't like withholding information from her. "He was married twice."

Kim nodded. "Yes, he admitted as much, but according to him he got a divorce in both situations. Are you saying that he didn't?"

"No, there were divorces."

Duan paused a moment. "Both women turned up missing during the marriage, and to this day have not been heard from."

Kim bit down on her lip and fought to keep her composure. "Are you saying what I think you are?"

He nodded. "Yes. On two occasions Edward was a suspect in his wives' disappearances. No one was able to prove foul play on his part because he had real good alibis."

Kim's eyes widened. "But if he *was* in some way responsible, that means…"

He knew what she was thinking, although it was apparently hard for her to say it out loud. "Yes," he said softly, gazing deep into her eyes. "That's what it means."

8

"OH, MY GOD." Kim closed her eyes and drew in a deep breath. She felt her body trembling at the same time she felt Duan's strong hands gently stroking her back.

"It's okay, Kim. Nothing is going to happen to your mother," he whispered in a deep, husky voice close to her ear. "I give you my word on that."

She shook her head. She heard his words but didn't fully understand how he could say them. In fact, a part of her brain refused to comprehend any of what he'd said. She was imagining things—yes, that had to be it. There was no way Duan had insinuated that the man her mother planned to marry could be responsible for the deaths of his previous two wives.

She opened her eyes and stared up into Duan's face, and knew from his expression that she hadn't imagined anything. It was true.

She wrenched away from him as anger consumed her. "And you've known this since that Sunday in Chicago when we shared a cab ride to the airport?" she asked in an accusing tone. "You knew what Edward Villarosas was capable of doing, yet you didn't tell me when you were aware my mother was spending time with him? Planning to marry him?" Cold, hard fear struck Kim in the chest at the very thought of Edward Villarosas and her mother together.

Duan knew Kim was upset. Highly pissed was more like it. He'd guessed what her reaction would be, which was why he hadn't told her sooner. Now that she knew, it was imperative that he convince her Wynona wasn't at risk and exactly what was at stake and why they needed to do things his way.

"The reason I didn't tell you as soon as you mentioned the name was because I had to verify we were talking about the same person."

"And when you discovered it was the same person?" she asked hotly, pressing the issue.

"Then it was a matter of acknowledging the first rule of law." He leaned against the wall and crossed his arms over his chest. "No matter how things might look, a person is innocent until proven guilty, and after two investigations, some of Atlanta's finest detectives couldn't come up with anything to nail Villarosas. He had ironclad alibis. He and his wives weren't even in the same cities when they disappeared."

"Then why on earth do you think he's guilty of anything?"

Duan knew it would be a waste of time to explain about a cop's intuition. Landon had only worked on the second case, but when he'd learned about the first, which happened a good five years before he'd become a cop, he'd tried making a connection but hadn't been able to do so. That didn't necessarily mean there wasn't one, but time and city budget cuts had prevented the force from following up on every plausible lead.

"A few things didn't add up," he heard himself saying. "But they weren't enough to get a conviction if we had wanted to take things that far."

He remembered the evidence wasn't even enough to get the man locked up for the night as a suspect. People had verified his whereabouts and the two incidents had been five years apart.

"But you just said he wasn't in the same cities as his wives when they disappeared." She was thoughtful a moment. "So what did Edward think happened to them? It is odd both wives disappeared."

"He said they were having affairs and left him for other men."

She lifted a brow. "I wonder if he realizes that doesn't make him look very good—as if he was lacking in certain areas."

"Yes, you could think that. But there were others who knew the women and claimed they definitely liked to flirt. The witnesses believed they were involved in affairs, though no one knew the names of the men."

Kim pushed a curl behind her ear. She still had a lot of questions but at least she had an answer to one of them, the one she'd asked herself just last week. Why would Duan want to come to Shreveport with her? She now saw that it had nothing to do with him enjoying her company, at least not to the extent she'd assumed. Men liked sex and she would be the first to admit that what was between them was off the charts. However, now that she was aware of his real motivation, she wouldn't be surprised to find out that he'd had his bags packed, ready to come here and nail Edward Villarosas, the moment she'd mentioned his name.

She glanced up to find Duan staring at her. "And you think you'll be able to crack a case—two cases—in one week? Do you honestly believe that Edward will give something away to make that happen?"

She watched as he dragged in a deep breath. "If cracking the cases was just dependent on me, then I would say no. But I'm not the only one working them. I have four other men in the firm who're just as determined to solve this, and I consider them the best there are. One is even a former FBI agent. The first thing we had to do was get the Atlanta police to agree to reopen the files. And now that that's been done, we have technical equipment at our disposal that wasn't on the market a few years ago. I feel certain if there was foul play in either case, we're going to find out this time. We have the time, manpower and the resources to do it."

Kim began pacing as she tried to make sense of everything Duan had said. Moments later, she stopped and glanced over at him.

He was leaning against the wall, arms crossed. His expression was unreadable, but she was certain hers showed that she was still upset.

Thinking she had paced long enough, she moved over to the sofa and sat down. "I gather there wasn't sufficient motive in either case. He couldn't collect on insurance policies since the women—according to him—weren't dead, just missing."

"True."

"So the only thing you and your friends have to go on is gut instincts?" When he lifted his brow, she said, "Yes, I know all about gut instincts. I dated a detective while living in D.C. It was a short-term affair but long enough to get an idea of how a cop thinks. That's one of the things he and I didn't agree on, because people in the medical field, we base our decisions on scientific data."

"And so do we, to a certain extent," he said. "The use of DNA proves that. But still, there are times when you know something doesn't add up, but you just can't prove it. And unfortunately, there're not always unlimited funds available to prove your theories. The city of Atlanta was undergoing budget cuts, so without evidence to support a lengthy investigation the cases stayed in missing persons and never made it over to homicide."

He paused to allow what he'd said to sink in before adding, "Landon Chestnut, the detective who originally worked the second case, felt something was missed in the first, which hindered him from doing a good job. Now he can pursue both with a full team behind him."

Duan finally moved away from the wall to take the chair across from Kim. He was fully aware that over the past twenty minutes or so, in the midst of their conversations, something was taking place between them that had nothing to do with sex but everything to do with trust. She was upset, understandably so, yet she'd been willing to listen while he explained things.

"I wish I could say that after meeting Villarosas I think Landon is wrong," he spoke up and said. "But before I flew out here I was able to read documentation on both cases, and I think there's more to it than two women deciding they no longer wanted to be married and hauling ass, never to be heard from again."

His opinion did nothing to relieve her anxiety. It only worsened it. "If what you say is true, then how can you think my mother's life is not in danger, Duan?"

He leaned forward and rested his elbows on his thighs. "First of all, if Villarosas has gotten rid of two wives, he wouldn't risk there being a third without raising a lot of suspicions. And he and your mother aren't married yet and he has no reason to think she's being unfaithful like the other two were. Besides that, he asked about my profession before we left your mother's house, so he knows I'm an ex-cop. He even knows I'm an ex-cop from Atlanta and he's probably wondering if I'm familiar with the investigation."

Kim sighed and leaned back in her chair. "But solving a case can take weeks, months, possibly years. You met my mother, Duan. You saw how her face lit up when Edward got there. She's fallen for him, and if he's not what he's pretending to be then she should know it and I'm the one who should tell her."

"If you were to tell her now, would she believe you? How do you know he hasn't already told her that he's had two wives run off and made it seem it was their choice? And would knowing that about him make your mother leery of him? In Wynona's mind, he's a good man, so unless you can present concrete evidence to the contrary, she'll take anything you say as an attempt to keep them apart."

Kim was silent for a while because what Duan had said was the truth. Her mother could very well know about Edward's two wives. She certainly hadn't reacted when he'd answered Duan's question earlier about whether he'd ever been married. He hadn't hesitated to admit to two divorces, so chances were he'd told her mother about his wives' disappearances, as well. Kim knew her mother wouldn't suspect Edward of any foul play.

"I can't let her marry him until I know for sure he's innocent, Duan," she said, glancing over at him.

He nodded. "And like I said earlier, with all five of us working the case, not to mention the detective with the Atlanta police department, I feel we should come up with something—even if nothing more than a motive."

"And then what?"

"And then we present what we have to the police, and to your mother. Until then, she won't believe mere speculation on our part." He leaned back in his chair. "There is no doubt in my mind that Villarosas is a manipulator. I watched your mother while he was talking. He's convinced her that he's the best thing since sliced bread."

Kim felt that was a pretty good assessment, one she'd made herself. "So what can we do?"

"Right now, nothing. My partners know how important it is that we determine once and for all what happened to those women, and if that means starting back at square one, then that's what we'll do."

His words didn't give Kim much comfort. What he was anticipating doing could take time, and time was something they didn't have, not when her mother intended to marry Edward in a few weeks.

"There has to be something we can do now," she said in a frustrated tone.

"There is. I need you to act as if he's winning you over. That's going to be important to him. I'm sure he's already figured out that he's rubbed me the wrong way, and he either doesn't give a damn or he's going to do his best to get on my good side, if for no other reason than to try to figure out what I know."

"Won't he become suspicious if he finds out the cases have been reopened?"

"Possibly. But he won't connect me to anything. In fact I'm going to make him believe I know nothing about it. I was up front with him about being a former police officer, and he's probably thinking I wouldn't have done so had I recognized his name."

He stood up and crossed over to her, reaching out his hand. She stared at it for a moment before placing her own hand in his. He tugged her to her feet, and when he wrapped his arms around her waist she made a feeble attempt to pull away. He tightened his hold, not letting her go.

"You should have told me," she said, narrowing her eyes at him.

He lifted her chin to connect their gazes. He couldn't help but see the hurt in the depths of her dark brown eyes and it was like a kick in the gut. He'd never meant to hurt her.

"Things had to be done this way, Kim. Any false move could blow up in our face—cause potential evidence to be thrown out. I can't risk him wiggling through any loopholes. Would you want that, especially if he's guilty?"

"No."

"Had I told you any sooner you would have caught the first plane here to confront both Villarosas and your mother, without any proof. That would only have pushed them closer together. They would have eloped before you could have stopped them. This way we both know what we have to do and we'll work together to nail him." He paused to let his words sink in.

"So, are we a team or not?" he asked after a few moments.

A part of Kim wanted to go somewhere and cry her eyes out. Finding out that the one man her mother believed could make her happy was a fake and possible murderer was bad enough. And then to be reminded that sex was the only thing between her and Duan, and that the only reason he was there was to work undercover—

"Kim?"

She tilted up her chin, scowling fiercely. "What?"

"Are we or are we not a team? Do we not want the same thing here?"

She sighed and looked up at him. "Yes, but I want to know everything I can about Villarosas and those two cases. Did you bring those reports with you?"

"Yes."

"Good, because I intend to read them. If Edward is innocent I'll be the first to apologize to him and Mom for doubting him, but if he's guilty of any crimes then I want to make sure he pays for what he's done."

9

KIM PUT DOWN the documents she'd been reading for the past hour and rubbed her eyes. As a nurse she was used to reports, some even thicker than the three-hundred-page document Duan had given her. However, most of them were medical in nature and reached a conclusion at the end, a diagnosis. Although a lot of information was documented from various sources in this investigative report, there was no definite finding.

"Here, looks like you can use this."

She smiled when Duan placed a cup of coffee in front of her. "Thanks."

He eased into the chair beside her. After she'd started to read the report he had pulled out a laptop. For the past hour they had worked in amiable silence, the only sounds in the room those of her turning pages and him clicking on the keyboard.

But the one thing she was constantly aware of was his presence. Just knowing he was there within arm's reach was a comforting thought. All she had to do was sniff the air to breathe in the manly scent of his aftershave. Occasionally she would glance over at him, see how intense he was, and she realized how seriously he took his job as a private investigator.

She'd never been a woman who needed or even desired to have a man underfoot, but having Duan here with her felt good. And knowing they were, as he called it, a team made it even better. After giving her the report, he had reminded her that he had asked her to consider him as a pretend fiancé *before* she'd mentioned Villarosas's name. That was the only comforting thought in this entire thing.

She took a sip of her coffee. It was good. Not for the first time, she wondered if there was anything Duan Jeffries wasn't good at. She glanced back down at the report, thinking he'd certainly made it easy for her to follow along. The highlighted sections might as well have been her own, and all the questions he'd jotted on sticky notes were the same ones she would have asked.

"Is the report boring you with all that investigative jargon?"

She glanced over at him. Earlier he had been sitting on the sofa with the computer in his lap. Now he had placed the laptop on the table to take a break and enjoy a cup of coffee with her. And he had changed clothes. He was wearing a pair of jeans and a T-shirt and he was in his bare feet. He looked at home. Sexy.

"No, I find all that stuff interesting and I'm amazed at how police officers and detectives can tie it all together and bring the case to a conclusion."

"Trust me, it's not always easy," he said, smiling over at her. "And in a lot of cases there are loose ends, things that don't add up."

She nodded. "Yes, I saw those."

"And the sad thing is that without time, resources and money, those loose ends are never thoroughly checked out. There are a number of them listed in the report, but without proof it all boils down to speculation."

"And a lot of legal loopholes to slip through."

He held her gaze for a moment, then nodded.

She gave a frustrated sigh, beginning to understand more about him and his work. A couple of weeks ago she'd asked him to tell her about himself, the good, the bad and the ugly. This had been his bad. The inability to right a wrong because of legal loopholes.

"I refuse to let this be one of them, Duan. I will never be satisfied until I know the truth about what really happened to those women, and we don't have months or years to find it out. There has to be something else we can do. Every day Mom is falling deeper and deeper in love with him, and I can't live my life with her here in Shreveport. Whether in the Keys or wherever I'll be living while in medical school, I'll be constantly wondering if she's safe or if Villarosas has decided to make her his next victim. If something has pushed him over the edge to make him want to harm her."

She stood and began pacing. "There is so much we don't know about him. So much that Mom doesn't know. Maybe we should go back there tonight and tell her that we've decided to stay at her place instead of at the hotel so we can keep an eye on things."

"And how do you suggest we explain our decision to do that without her getting suspicious of anything?" he asked.

She slid her hands into the back pockets of her jeans and threw her head back. "Do you have any better ideas?" she snapped.

This woman knew how to pump up his adrenaline, Duan thought, for the good and for the bad. He felt her anger, he understood her frustration and knew her mother was her main concern. And knowing that, he would deal with anyone who dared to hurt her or someone she cared about. Mainly because he was beginning to feel this connection to her that he didn't want to feel.

He stood and moved toward her and she gave him a look that all but said, *Don't mess with me.* He shrugged. She was a spitfire and was having one of her moments. He would help her through it.

He came to a stop in front of her. "Yes, I have a few ideas that we can discuss in detail later. Most of them involve those blue sticky notes I've placed throughout the report. But right now I think you need to chill and work off some anger. I'm going to help you do that."

She rolled her eyes. "I bet. And how do you plan to accomplish that?" she asked with a look that said quite simply that whatever he had in mind, now was not the time to try it.

Duan smiled, reading her thoughts and knowing her assumptions were wrong. "Give me a couple of minutes and I'll have things ready for you," he said, moving away and heading toward the bedroom.

Kim looked confused. "Have what ready for me? Where are you going?"

He turned and a smile touched the corners of his lips. "You need to be pampered so I'm going into the bathroom to prepare your bubble bath."

KIM SANK DOWN DEEPER in the tub beneath all the bubbles and closed her eyes. No man had ever prepared a bath for her. Duan had done more than just run the bathwater; he had made her feel special. And what she found so amazing was that he probably wasn't even aware he'd done so. Certain kinds of deeds seemed to be an ingrained part of his nature. She figured it had to have come from being the oldest and looking out for his younger siblings. Although she couldn't imagine him ever being Terrence's keeper, Olivia was a different matter.

When she'd come to the Keys to be fitted for their bridesmaid dresses, Olivia had told her and Sherri that both of her brothers had been overprotective while she was growing up, Duan more so than Terrence. There were some things she could pull over on Terrence that she wouldn't dare try with Duan. Kim could believe that.

Kim breathed in the scented bubbles as she thought about her mother. More than anything she wished there weren't so many unanswered questions in the hundred or so pages she'd already read on that first case involving Edward. With all the evidence and eyewitnesses interviewed, no one would have reason to suspect foul play of any kind.

It seemed that Mandy Villarosas had been a bona fide flirt. Even the girlfriends with whom she'd gone away for the weekend had verified she had met some man in the club the night before she disappeared.

That was close to ten years ago, before video cameras were used in most businesses. After reading that report one could almost sympathize with Edward for having a wife with loose morals.

But what she wanted to gather from the reports— and she still had the second case to read—was whether there were similarities between the two women, physical or emotional. And more important, whether there were similarities between her mother and the two women. People became serial killers for any number of reasons.

She shuddered at the thought that Villarosas was a serial killer, but until he was cleared of all suspicions, she would do everything within her power to make sure her mother didn't marry the man.

"Time's up."

Kim opened her eyes and glanced over at Duan. He was standing in the doorway with a huge bath towel in his hand. "But, it's only been—"

"Almost an hour. Look at the bubbles."

She did. Most were gone. Talk about not having any staying power. "I'm disappointed. I thought you would be joining me," she said, easing her body to sit up straight. "The tub's big enough."

"Yes, but you needed this time to yourself."

She agreed that she had needed the time. He was thoughtful not only knowing it but making it happen. "I'm still worried about Mom, Duan."

He nodded as he slowly walked toward her and the hot tub. "Sure you are. You wouldn't be the daughter that you are if you weren't. Your mother has always meant a lot to you."

And yours meant a lot to you until you learned to stop caring, to shield the pain, Kim wanted to say. But she didn't. Instead, when he reached the edge of the tub and opened the huge velour towel, she unashamedly stood up and he wrapped the towel around her before effortlessly lifting her out.

He placed her on her feet and began toweling her dry, patting her wet skin. Never had she felt so taken care of. She could get used to this kind of attention.

A part of her wanted to tell him that she could do it herself, but she didn't. She liked the feel of his touch. And she especially liked his tender ministrations as he gently stroked every inch of her flesh. So she stood there while he took his time drying her wet shoulders, all around her breasts and down to her stomach.

He bent down in front of her to dry her hips and thighs before gently patting dry the curls between them. She watched him and saw how long his lashes were, then noted that his breathing had changed. Without warning he grabbed one of his T-shirts and pulled it over her head, working her arms through the sleeves. It was then that he swept her off her feet and into his arms.

"Where are you taking me?" she asked, looking up at him, studying the jaw that she found so fascinating.

He looked down at her from beneath those long lashes. "The living room. I want to hold you for a while."

A part of her wanted to protest and say she didn't need to be held. And that she didn't want any man to assume she was a weakling that needed his attention. When he lowered his body on the sofa and cuddled her into his arms, for a moment she stared up at him, and he stared back. Then she snuggled closer to him, her head coming to rest against the warmth of his broad chest, and she could actually feel the beating of his heart beneath her cheek.

She closed her eyes thinking that yes, she liked being held by him.

DUAN THOUGHT THERE was something just plain sensual about a woman who was comfortable within her own skin. A woman who knew what she wanted and didn't mind going after it, no matter what it was.

He stood by the bed glancing down at Kim. She was a woman who embraced her sexuality like she had every right to do so, a woman so damn beautiful that his eyes were feeling sore just looking at her.

She had fallen asleep in his arms and he figured she would rest better in the bed. But for a while he had simply enjoyed holding her, listening to her even breathing. It was a peaceful slumber, one he had helped make possible, and he was pleased with that.

Over the years he'd had affairs with many women, but he could now say, quite truthfully, he'd never been involved with one as bold, brazen and gorgeous as this one. But then tonight, she had surrendered to his care and he had enjoyed pampering her, trying to ease her stress and tension. In a way, he wanted her to know that with him she could lighten whatever load she was carrying.

She was worried about her mother and he knew that. And he was well aware that if she could do so, she would pack up and go stay at Wynona's home for the rest of the trip. But he knew that wouldn't be a smart move since they needed to convey as much normalcy in their relationship as possible so Villarosas wouldn't suspect anything. Like he'd told Kim, they were now a team.

A team.

For some reason he liked the sound of that. While on the police force he'd had a female partner once. A very competent woman who was good at what she did, and he'd always felt secure that she was covering his back. But he and Kim were a different kind of team. He felt a bond with her that he couldn't explain but knew existed.

She shifted position in bed and the ring she wore drew his attention. The ring he'd placed there earlier that day. He felt a sudden tightness in his chest. Seeing that ring—his ring—on her hand did something to him.

He never wanted to see it on anyone else's hand.

Sweet mercy. He rubbed his hands down his face, knowing what that admission meant. For all his bantering about how he never wanted to share his life with any woman, he knew if the circumstances were different, if she didn't have dreams to pursue, he would make her a permanent part of his life. He could honestly say that he had never wanted a woman as badly as he wanted her. And that intense desire had originated the first time he'd set eyes on her.

He had been drawn to her because deep down, in spite of all the sexual chemistry they generated, there had been another pull just as strong.

They were alike in a number of ways. Both had parental issues they couldn't let go of. Her father and his mother had turned them off ever having a fulfilling marriage of their own. But he could now say that the thought of settling down and committing his life to a woman didn't scare the hell out of him like it once had, and he credited that to Kim. She was nothing like Susan Jeffries, and he believed she would never desert the man she loved or the children she'd given birth to. She was loyal and dedicated to a fault. Definitely the kind of woman any man would want to claim as his own.

And the thought of any man doing that was something he didn't want to think about.

10

KIM TRIED TO FEIGN SLEEP at the feel of a hard erection poking her in the back, dead center where her butt cheeks came together, and a hot wet tongue gliding across the skin at her nape.

She closed her eyes and decided she wasn't ready to let Duan know she was awake yet. She curled her hands into fists when he shifted and his tongue began moving down her spine.

"Since you're awake, how about flipping on your back so we can play," a deep husky voice said, his heated breath sending sensuous sensations uncoiling in her belly.

She smiled and glanced over her shoulder before turning onto her back. "How did you know I was awake?"

He looked up into her face. "By the way you were breathing. I didn't touch you until I knew I had your attention. You didn't fool me."

And before she could make a comment to that, he shifted his body and leaned down to kiss her. The first thing that came to her mind was that his tongue was full of energy this morning, and the second was that she didn't have one single complaint about it, especially after the way he'd pampered her last night.

She so loved the feel of his mouth on hers, the way he seemed to put everything into every kiss they shared. And how he seemed to greedily lap her up, feast hungrily on her as he drove his tongue deeper and deeper inside her mouth.

The ringing of her cell phone had them breaking apart, sucking in hard breaths. "That's probably Mom making sure we don't forget breakfast," she said, shifting to reach for the ringing phone.

Before she got too far away, Duan reached out, grabbed a thigh and leaned down to place a kiss right in the center of her stomach before sliding off the bed and grabbing his own cell phone off the nightstand. He had heard the humming sound as it vibrated before daybreak, but had decided to miss the call since he didn't want to wake Kim.

He saw the missed call had come from Landon. While Kim chatted with her mother he moved toward the balcony to return Landon's call. "Hey, man, what's up?"

"Just wanted to check in to see if you've met Villarosas yet."

"Yes, I met him and you were right. He seems like an arrogant ass. How is Chevis doing with the first case?"

"He's trying to find out the identity of the man Mandy Villarosas was supposed to have flirted with that night at the club. Chev is convinced someone might remember something."

"Even after ten years?"

"Yes. According to the report taken from one of the women, a class reunion party was also going on at the club that night, which means there was probably a lot of picture-taking. Chev is going to track down some of the partygoers to see if he can gather photos. I'll let you know what we find out."

Duan ended the call and flipped off the phone as he reentered the hotel room. He glanced over at Kim. She returned his gaze with troubled eyes. It was obvious something was wrong.

"Are you okay?" he asked.

She shrugged her shoulders. "Yes, I guess. I just finished talking to Mom and she sounded so happy and excited." She laughed bitterly and a fiery look appeared in her eyes. "It pisses me off that the man that has brought so much joy to her life could end up being a damn murderer."

Duan knew how she felt, but he also knew they needed to play the game well with Villarosas, which meant perfecting their acting abilities. "Forget the personal now, Kim. Put a lid on the anger. We need to concentrate on nailing this guy if he's guilty, and the only way we can do that is to find out everything there is to know. We've come this far and the last thing we need is to have my cover blown. Villarosas has to believe he has us snowed, especially you. You can't in any way let him know you suspect something. The questions you ask him should be the same ones you would ask any man about to marry your mother. And you want to make him feel comfortable in telling you anything you want to know."

He reached out and traced the line of her jaw with his fingertips. "Can you do that, Kim? If you can't, I'll understand. No questions asked. No explanation required. But a lot is at stake and—"

"I can do it, Duan," she said with clear certainty and unwavering confidence. "And I *will* do it. If he isn't what Mom thinks he is, then I need to help expose him. We're not doing this just for my mother. I have to remember the families of those other two women who don't know if they're alive somewhere or really dead. I have to do it for them, too."

He smiled and cupped her jaw before lowering his mouth down to hers. The moment their lips touched, a fiery heat exploded within his gut and he slid his tongue inside her mouth, tangled with hers, and laved the insides from corner to corner. And when she wrapped her arms around his neck he dropped his hand from her jaw and slid it around her waist.

Her body melted into his and he could only continue to kiss this woman who affected him like no other. The woman responsible for making him want things he never wanted before. The woman who made it possible for him to consider all the possibilities, but only with her.

She was one and done. If he could not have her, then he would not have anyone, because he was convinced she was his other half, the one that made him whole. He was letting his emotions come into play and get the best of him, but he couldn't do anything to stop it.

Reluctantly, he pulled his mouth away and pressed his forehead against hers. There was so much passion between them. How could that be possible?

He took a step back. "I was just talking to Landon and he indicated that Chevis is in Orlando following up a possible lead. The report you read indicated that the night before Mandy Villarosas, wife number one, disappeared there was a party at the club—a high-school reunion."

Kim nodded. "Yes, I recall reading that in the report."

"As with most reunions, there're always people taking a lot of pictures at random. We're contacting a few of the attendees to see if someone got a shot of this man—the person Mandy supposedly flirted with that night. The women she went out of town with that weekend think he's the same man that she was to meet the day she disappeared."

Kim frowned. "But if that's true and there is a possibility there was another man involved, then..."

She stopped talking, hoping Duan was following her train of thoughts. He was.

"That means if there was another man involved, then that man could very well be the person behind her disappearance," Duan replied. "Remember, we've never said Villarosas is guilty of any crime, but he is under suspicion."

"With the scenario you just presented, I don't know how he can be a suspect, Duan. What if the man at the club is the same man she went to meet? He would be the main suspect, wouldn't he?"

Duan nodded. "Yes and no. There're still a lot of gray areas. That's why we're looking into all the possibilities. Just remember, it wasn't the first case that roused Landon's suspicions because he never worked that one. It was the second case and now we have access to both. And we're going to proceed as if Edward is innocent until proven guilty, or at least until we can establish a motive."

"And if Mom insists on marrying him before then?"

"Then we'll level with her and tell her our suspicions. But as I told you, chances are she might not want to believe that he's capable of harming anyone. And you need to apprise me of everyone your mother might be inviting to the breakfast this morning so there won't be any surprises. I don't want to be caught off guard about anything. You can school me on the drive over."

"Okay."

"And remember, no matter what, we're a team."

She smiled. "I'll remember."

Duan glanced at the clock on the wall. "Ready to take a shower?" he asked, heading in the direction of the bathroom.

"You go ahead, I need to call the hospital and check on someone who came through E.R. Thursday, a little boy who'd gotten bitten by a poisonous snake. They were flying in the anti-venom and I want to see how he's doing."

"Okay." He turned to enter the bathroom and then stopped to look back at her. As if he needed to taste her again, he walked over and pulled her into his arms, covering her mouth with his.

Unlike the one earlier, this kiss was unexpected, spontaneous, and sensations immediately flooded Kim's body. The breath she'd been about to take was reduced to a shudder. His tongue was making a quick but thorough study of her mouth and the tip of his finger was making erotic circles on her back. She needed this. She wanted this. And he was giving it to her in perfect measure, using his tongue to stroke her into tranquility, to give her the peace and calm she needed at that moment.

Reluctantly, he pulled back and released her. He held her gaze for a moment, and then without saying a single word he crossed the room to the bathroom and closed the door behind him.

11

"SO, HOW DID YOU AND Kim meet?"

Duan smiled down at Aunt Gert, who appeared to be in her early sixties. Kim had warned him that her aunt would ask a lot of questions. And she was right.

Breakfast had become a Saturday-morning brunch outside on the terrace. Wynona and Aunt Gert had done most of the cooking, and Duan had to agree the women were great cooks. He couldn't help noticing that Edward had avoided him most of the morning, but was in Kim's face every chance he got.

"Kim and I met when her best friend Sherri, whom I'm sure you know, became engaged to my brother Terrence," he answered truthfully.

"So, was it love at first sight?" Aunt Gert asked with a hopeful look on her face.

He was inclined to agree with her on that. "Let's just say there were a lot of things about Kim that drew me to her. Things I definitely liked and admired." He took a sip of iced tea. Kim had said her Aunt Gert was a die-hard romantic and she was right. The woman was really taking this all in.

He glanced across the room at Kim. She was talking to a man she had introduced earlier as her mother's neighbor, Benjamin Sanders, whom she fondly called Mr. Bennie.

Duan suddenly realized just how true the statement was that he'd made to Aunt Gert. There had been a number of things he'd liked about Kim right off the bat. Her looks headed the list, of course. But it didn't take long to discover that she was a very intelligent woman who had a profound sense of caring for others, and he hadn't been surprised to learn she was a nurse. Another thing he liked about her was her spunk.

"Well, I'm just glad she finally got serious about a man. For a while, I was concerned about her."

"Concerned?" he asked.

"Yes, concerned."

Duan chuckled at the elderly woman's words. "You were concerned that she hadn't gotten serious about a man?"

"Yes, after all, she's twenty-seven."

"Yes, ma'am."

"In today's society, if a woman her age doesn't have a man, people start to think things," Aunt Gert said.

"Is that why you sent her résumé to that television show—because you were concerned whether she even *liked* men?" he asked incredulously, having caught on to what Aunt Gert was insinuating.

She met his gaze. "Yes."

At that moment he would have thought unkindly of the woman if he hadn't seen all the love she felt for Kim radiating in her face. "Trust me, no one has to wonder about Kim. She's all the woman any man would ever want or need." And he knew all the way to the base of his groin that statement was true.

The woman's face lit up in a smile. "I'm glad to hear it. And I like that ring you've put on her finger. It looks just like it belongs there."

Duan couldn't help but smile himself. "Yes, I think so, as well. So rest assured, Aunt Gert. My woman is doing just fine."

He took a slow sip of his lemonade. *My woman.* His thoughts floated back to that morning. She had indeed been *his* woman. He hadn't expected her to join him in the shower, but once she'd found out the little boy was recovering from the snake bite, she had. Together they had given the word *steam* a whole new meaning. One that made sensations stir from his chest to his groin just thinking about it.

His gaze sought Kim out across the room. Someone had placed a baby in her arms, one of her cousins' babies, he assumed. She looked like a natural holding it, and then he recalled that she'd told him she wanted children one day, but didn't intend to marry. He continued to look at her and doubted if his own mother had ever had such a look on her face while holding him, Terrence or Olivia.

"Well, I've consumed enough of your time, Duan. Wynona is hoping that everyone will hang around for dinner because she's fixing a feast. I'll go see if she needs help with anything in the kitchen."

When she walked off, he felt someone looking at him and met Edward Villarosas's gaze. He was standing with a group of men but his attention was on Duan. Deciding the man had avoided him long enough that day, Duan crossed the room when the men Edward had been talking to walked off.

"So, Edward, how are things going?" Duan asked.

Edward smoothed his hand over his bald head. "Fine. I see that you're fitting in rather nicely."

Duan chuckled. "I'm trying to. Tell me," he said, meeting Edward's gaze, "was it easy for you?"

"To do what?"

"Fit in."

"Oh, sure. Wynona has nice relatives." Edward hesitated a moment then said, "So, you were a cop in Atlanta. I lived in Atlanta for a while. For ten years."

Duan widened his eyes as if he were surprised by the statement. "That's a long time. Why did you leave?"

Edward shrugged. "After my divorces there was nothing there for me anymore. I wanted a fresh start so I moved here." After taking a sip of his lemonade he asked, "How long were you a cop?"

"Seven years," Duan said.

"Were you always on the beat?" Edward asked.

Duan shook his head. "No, I made detective after my second year. After doing detective work for a number of years, I decided to get my own private investigative firm. I'm proud to say I'm doing well with it."

"That's good to hear."

"What about you? What did you do for a living while in Atlanta?"

"I was a mechanic for a long time and had my own shop, mostly working on antique cars."

"Really?" Duan said, as if he hadn't known that fact. "What was the name of it?"

"Villarosas Auto Shop. It was located in College Park."

The man glanced around the room. "Excuse me, Duan, but I need to go see Wynona for a second." Duan watched him head outside to the patio.

"How are things going?"

He glanced up and saw that Kim had approached. "Okay. What about with you?"

"Edward is asking a lot of questions."

"About what?"

"You. And I hope I gave him all the right answers."

Duan frowned. "What sort of questions?"

"Questions I'd assume a father would ask when his daughter brought a guy to the house for their first date. How long were you a cop? Are you a detective, and if so, how long? Where did you live in Atlanta and for how long? Those sorts of questions."

Duan nodded. "And what did you tell him?"

"What we agreed that I would."

"Good. I might add you to my P.I. firm yet," he teased, leaning toward her and placing a kiss on her lips. Anyone looking at them would assume they were sharing a loving moment.

She chuckled. "No, thank you. I'll stick to the medical field. Anyway, I think I surprised him when I finally told him that considering he was going to marry my mom, the two of you should get to know each other. And that if he wanted to know anything else about you, he needed to ask you himself."

Duan smiled. "He did, but I'm sure more questions are coming later."

He placed his arm around her shoulder and tried to downplay the tingle he felt in his gut from touching her. No matter where she'd been in the room all morning, he'd been aware of her.

"How did things go with you and Aunt Gert?" she asked.

"I think she likes me."

"How was the rest of your day with Edward?" Duan asked. "I couldn't help noticing a few times he had you stuck in a corner all to himself." It was later that evening and they were heading back toward the hotel, momentarily stuck in traffic as a train passed.

Kim glanced over and gave him a faint smile. Everyone had hung around for dinner and afterward several people played a game of cards. Duan was right. Edward had participated in one or two games, but most of the time he'd cornered her. She wasn't surprised Duan had noticed. In fact, she had picked up on him watching her a lot that day. And knowing his gaze was on her had given her sensuous shivers. The thought that he had that effect on her no longer came as a surprise.

"Yes, I did everything you'd suggested and kept him talking. He didn't say a lot about his marriages, but he did tell me he didn't have any kids and that was his one regret in life. So, he's looking forward to becoming my stepfather." She sighed. "That's basically it. And he did talk about how happy he plans on making Mom. So, what did you find out?"

"Not a whole lot. He likes playing golf and going fishing. He suggested we do both while I'm here. Of course I didn't turn down the opportunity to spend more time with him. I also got him to talk about his past life in Atlanta. But other than telling me about the auto mechanic shop he used to own in College Park, he was rather tight-lipped."

"That doesn't tell us a lot, does it?" Kim asked.

"No. However, as days go on—"

"But that's just it, Duan. Instead of spending time getting to know the man my mother is marrying for the right reasons, I'm questioning him for all the wrong ones, only because—"

"I know what you're about to say, Kim, and I understand. But—"

"Does there have to be a *but,* Duan?"

"In this case, yes. Now tell me about your mom's neighbor."

She glanced over at him in surprise. "Who? Mr. Bennie?"

"Yes."

"Why would you want to know anything about him?"

"He seems to like your mom."

Kim rolled her eyes. "Of course he likes Mom. They've lived next door to each other for years and have known each other even longer. They attended school together. The house Mom is living in now used to be my grandparents' house and the house Mr. Bennie lives in used to be his parents' house, so he and Mom were neighbors growing up. He's a few years older than she is."

She shifted a little in her seat to look at Duan. "When his mother died, Mr. Bennie and his wife and only daughter moved back to Shreveport to take care of his father. But his dad only lived a year after that. And around eight years ago, Mr. Bennie's wife, Ms. Diana, died of breast cancer."

Duan nodded, thinking the house Mr. Bennie was living in had experienced a lot of sadness. "Where's his daughter?"

"Valerie, who is a year older than I am, left for college in New Jersey and met a guy there. Now they're married with a little girl. I get to see them when I come home for Christmas. She usually comes and spends the holidays with Mr. Bennie like I do with Mom every year."

"He's never remarried?"

"No, he never remarried. I like Mr. Bennie. He's a really nice man who helps Mom out a lot with the yard and by doing odds and ends around the house."

Kim didn't say anything for a moment, then asked, "Why do you think he likes Mom *that* way?"

Duan smiled. "There are little things I notice, things I can now recognize as signs. Trust me when I say they went past me with my own father. And they went past Terrence, as well. Olivia pointed them out to us and made us aware that Cathy, our dad's secretary, had been in love with him for years. We thought Libby was crazy until she told us to pay more attention, so we did. At first we didn't pick up on anything, but then we noticed the looks Cathy would give Dad when he wasn't looking and how she would do anything for him."

"And you saw Mr. Bennie looking at Mom when he thought she wasn't looking?"

"Yes. And then there's the way his face lights up whenever she walks into a room. Trust me. I'd say he's definitely smitten. And sometimes people have a tendency not to notice someone who's always there, even if that person's the best thing for them."

At that moment, Duan's cell phone went off. Luckily they were still stalled in traffic, so he lifted his hip to pull the phone from his belt clip.

"Yes, Landon. What's up?"

"We may have found the guy in question. One of the women recognized him from some of the photos as the same guy Mandy Villarosas flirted with that night."

Duan nodded. "Did anyone recognize him as a former classmate?"

"No. So now we have a face, but we need a name. Brett is going to provide that."

Duan chuckled. Brett could do just about anything with a computer. "Let me know when he finds out something."

He clicked off the phone and glanced over at Kim. "We have a make on the guy that Mandy Villarosas was supposed to have met."

"So you know who he is?" she asked, not hiding her excitement.

"No, but he was captured in several pictures, so at least that's a start. We're not sure if he went there with someone, or if he knew anyone at the club. Remember, this was ten years ago."

Her hope deflated, Kim sank back into her seat. "So it will be like pulling a needle out of a haystack."

Duan laughed. "Not really. Especially since Brett is working that end of things."

"Brett? One of the guys in your firm?"

"Yes."

"Why?"

"Brett is our computer and technical expert and he's developed this high-tech network. All he has to do is scan in this guy's picture and it'll be distributed to all his databases. It goes to probably every law enforcement agency in the country, as well as the FBI's database. I'll give him less than forty-eight hours to find out the identity of the man."

"But like you said, it's been ten years," she reminded him.

"Yes, and the beauty of the equipment Brett has developed is that it can do an age enhancement. If we know what he looked like then, you can be certain we'll know what he looks like now. Brett has had quite a few successes."

"Wow."

Duan chuckled. "Yes, now we're getting somewhere."

He shifted his head to look out the windshield. It was dark and they were on a two-lane road with cars in front and back of them, all at a standstill. "Hell, how long is that train? It seems like we've been stopped for a while."

"Not sure. I told you to go this way because it's a short cut back to the hotel. I forgot about the train crossing."

He glanced back over at her and grinned. "Are you anxious to get back to the hotel?"

"Aren't you?"

Duan leaned back in his seat. "Yes."

"Why? You can't be hungry since my mother fed you plenty. What's the rush?"

The smile on his lips widened. "I'm surprised you have to ask, and it's probably the same reason as yours," he said throatily.

"You think?"

"I know. This is our third weekend together, Kim."

She was surprised he remembered. She thought only women recalled things like that. "And you want to celebrate?"

"Yeah, something like that."

She released her seat belt and edged closer to him on the bench seat. "Why wait until we get back to the hotel? We can start things right here."

"There is the matter of all these cars," he pointed out.

"Yes, but no one is beside us and it's dark. It will be like this for a while. So to my way of thinking we don't have to wait until we get back to the hotel to do certain things."

He swallowed deeply as she reached across his lap to push the button that slid their seats back.

He raised a brow. "Just what do you think you're doing?"

"You'll see."

He watched as her fingers pulled his zipper down. He had started getting hard the moment she mentioned them getting back to the hotel room.

"Kim, don't you think—"

"Shh. I don't think, Duan, and I don't want you to think, either. I just want you to relax and enjoy. And be a little daring."

And while she had been saying those words, she had slowly worked his shaft from his jeans. It was standing straight up and almost hitting the steering wheel.

"Gosh, you're an impressive man," she said, licking her lips while working her hands over his erection. And then before he could stop her, she dipped her head to his lap and took him into the warmth of her mouth.

"Kim!"

He called out her name but by now stopping her was a lost cause. He watched her head bob up and down and his entire groin ached at the feel of her mouth on him.

He felt hot, ready to explode, from the head of his penis all the way to his balls. Every lick of her tongue was pushing him slowly and deliciously over the edge. And every long, slow suck was almost causing him to come. He was tempted…boy, was he tempted, to fill her mouth with his release. If only she knew what she did to him. All the pleasure she was lavishing on him. Not just with her mouth, but with every part of her.

He let out a deep groan, thinking if he had to get stuck in traffic, then this was the best way to pass the time. The woman was definitely something else. He almost cursed when he saw the train's flashing last car, which meant they would be moving again soon.

"Kim?"

She didn't answer but continued feasting on him as if it were her last meal. She kept licking and went right on sucking and then he couldn't hold back.

"Kim!"

He came hard. Busting a nut had never been so spectacular, so damn fantastic. He tried to get a grip but it was too late. His body exploded and every nerve erupted. He tightened his hand on the steering wheel as electricity rushed through every part of him, and through it all her mouth did not let go of him. She kept it locked down on him as white fire spread through him, touching every cell in his body.

He moved a hand from the steering wheel to rub through the curls on her head, gently tugging, trying to pull her away from him. But she wouldn't let up, so he let her have her way as intoxicating sensations continued to rush through him. She had a way of satisfying every needy bone in his body and her sense of giving overwhelmed him.

When he had nothing left to give and she kept her mouth on him anyway, he whispered in a hoarse voice, "Kim, sweetheart, the train's gone by. You have to stop. The cars will start moving in a minute."

She lifted her head and looked up at him, holding his rod just mere inches from her wet lips. "You sure that's it?"

She was amazing. "For now. But when I get you back to the hotel…"

"What are you going to do?"

"You'll see." The blasting of a horn behind them signaled it was time to put the car in gear and move forward.

After tucking his shaft back inside and zipping his jeans, she returned to her seat, all the while licking her lips. "That was good."

"Mercy," he said, putting the car in gear and easing on the gas pedal. He was grateful to hit a traffic light. He needed to get his senses back in control. His shaft was still throbbing, but he knew that had to have been the most marvelous thing he'd ever experienced.

He glanced over at her. "I'm going to get you for that, Kim," he warned in a husky voice that rumbled deep from his gut.

She smiled at him sweetly. "You were going to *get* me anyway, weren't you, Duan?"

What she'd said was true, and the mere thought of it increased the throbbing in his groin. This was crazy. You would think after what she'd just done to him, his shaft would be satisfied for days.

The traffic light changed and the car moved forward. He couldn't wait to get her back to the hotel.

12

"YOU DO KNOW this is the third weekend straight that we've shared Sunday-morning breakfast in bed," Duan said, glancing over at Kim as he took a sip of his coffee.

Wearing a bathrobe, Kim sat cross-legged in the middle of the bed. She smiled over at him. "If we keep this up it might become one of those hard habits to break."

Duan placed his cup aside and leaned over to kiss her with a passion that Kim felt all the way to her toes.

After he pulled away she stared at him for long moments before saying, "Mom is going to call us when she and Edward are ready to head over to the county fair. In the meantime, what do you think we should do while we're waiting?"

He shook his head and chuckled. "Get the hell out of this room before we kill ourselves. I've had more sex with you in the past twenty-four hours than I've had all year."

She glanced away, nervously fiddling with the belt around her bathrobe. There was that word again. *Sex.* Was that all they'd been sharing for the past three weeks? When did a man stop thinking of it as nothing more than sex?

Evidently for Duan, it wouldn't be any time soon. But then, why should it? Just because she had started dealing with a bunch of crazy emotions was no reason to think he was doing the same.

Of their own accord her eyes skimmed down the muscular plane of his chest, reminding her how much she liked rubbing her fingers over it.

Kim forced herself to look at his face. "Is that what you want to do? Get out of the room?" she asked nervously, her tongue licking her top lip.

He stared at her. "No. Especially not when you do something like that with your tongue," he said in a voice so deep and sexy it made her shiver.

And then, as if he intended to make her do more than shiver, he raked his gaze from her lips down the rest of her body, taking in everything in his path, making her feel naked even while wearing her robe. The look in his eyes hinted at more than lust; it showed a hunger so hot that parts of her felt as if she were on fire.

Duan was about to lean forward to cop another kiss when his cell phone went off. He reached over toward the nightstand. "Whatever thoughts you were thinking, hold them until after I take this call."

He answered the phone. "This is Duan."

"Hey. Brett's been busy."

Duan smiled. That could only mean one thing. "What did he find?"

"Our man."

"Who is he?"

"His name is Stein Green and at the moment he's serving time in a Florida prison for armed robbery that involved the death of a police officer. It's pretty safe to say that Green will be behind bars for a while—he's serving a life sentence with no chance of parole. Chevis is on his way to Florida as we speak."

Duan nodded. "Let me know when Chevis finds out anything."

Moments later, he hung up the phone and glanced over at Kim. She looked gorgeous, even when she was sitting there staring at him expectantly.

"That was Landon," he said. "Brett has ID'd that guy—the one in the photos."

She nodded. "And?"

"And he's serving time for armed robbery in a jail in Florida. Chevis is on his way to pay him a visit."

Kim propped herself against one of the pillows. That was his favorite position. Well…one of his favorites. He much preferred seeing her on her back.

"That's good news," she said. "Do you think he'll tell him anything?"

"It depends. But I do know if there's one man who can get information out of someone, it's Chevis."

He eased off the bed. "Now is a good time for us to go over those case files since you've read both reports."

Kim watched him move across the room to get the reports from the table. He was only wearing a pair of briefs and she couldn't help thinking, not for the first time, that the man was built. Her gaze traveled up his sturdy long legs, flat tummy and broad chest. And his tush could make a woman drool, especially when he was wearing tight jeans.

She glanced at the digital clock on the nightstand. Her mother had gone to church and they would be getting together with her and Edward to go to the county fair around two.

Kim sighed. They had spent the entire day with her mother and the family yesterday, and intended to do the same for the remaining days she would be in Shreveport.

The thought of Wynona spending any time alone with Edward still bothered her, but she couldn't make a flap about it or it might push her mother even deeper into the man's arms. Edward Villarosas was certainly a charmer, or at least he tried to be.

She was supposed to leave next Sunday. She hoped, if nothing else, she could convince her mother to postpone her wedding plans for a while. She certainly intended to try.

KIM STEPPED AWAY from the car and glanced around. She recalled how each year when a county fair came to

New Orleans, she'd looked forward to going. That was the only time her father actually acted like a normal human being.

He had enjoyed taking her and her mother, and before their eyes he would transform into another person. It was as if he'd needed—if only for a little while—the chance to act like a kid again. He would head for the roller coasters first, which was probably the reason she'd inherited a fondness for the daring rides.

Her mother, who'd come to stand beside her, smiled and then leaned down and kissed her cheek. As if she knew what she'd been thinking, Wynona said, "I know you don't want to hear this, Kimani, but your father wasn't all bad."

Kim rolled her eyes. Her mother was right; she really didn't want to hear it. She glanced over and saw Duan and Edward standing by the car talking. The conversation appeared to be going well. She turned back to her mom. It wasn't the first time Wynona had tried convincing her of her father's goodness, so it wouldn't be the first time she'd had a problem believing it.

"Your father had a rough childhood," her mother went on to say.

"Please, Mom, give me a break. The man used to beat the crap out of you all the time."

"Yes, but only after he'd been drinking," her mother said defensively.

"Then that was almost every Friday night," Kim said. She really wasn't in the mood to rehash this bit of family history.

"Please remember those other days when he would be the fun, caring husband that I married."

Kim didn't say anything but a tightness in her stomach pushed her to ask, "Do you know where he is and do you ever hear from him?"

From the look on her mother's face Kim knew the answer. "You *do* know where he is and you *do* hear from him, don't you?" she asked in what she knew was an accusing voice.

Her mother didn't back down. "Yes to both, and the only reason he hasn't contacted you is because he's afraid you wouldn't accept him, and that would truly break his heart."

Kim frowned. "And I'm supposed to care about breaking his heart?"

Instead of answering, her mother rushed on, "He's your father and he has gotten help over the years."

"Good for him."

"Kim, listen, we—"

"No, Mom," she whispered so her voice wouldn't carry to the men. "When it comes to my father, there is no *we*. I don't hate him. I won't waste that much energy. He has to come to terms with how he treated you. Treated us."

"He never hit you."

"No, Mom, he didn't have to. He had you for his punching bag."

"But he's gotten better over the years. He's even in the church now."

Kim twirled her finger in the air and simultaneously rolled her eyes. "Whoop-de-do."

"Kim."

"Just what do you want from me, Mom?"

"I want you to find it in your heart to forgive your father. You've made the first step by finding a man to love, but before you can really move on you're going to have to forgive him. I had to do so and that's why I can get on with my life. He's a part of my past that I won't repeat. I've found someone who wants to make me happy."

"You sure of that?"

"Yes. Edward is a good man."

Kim bit down on her lower lip so she would not respond. A part of her hoped and prayed Duan and his partners were wrong about Edward and that he was a good man like her mother assumed. But she wasn't holding out for that. Duan had gone over the cases with her earlier, and she had a good idea how an investigator's mind worked. No stone would be left uncovered this time around.

She and her mother ended the conversation when they saw Edward and Duan approaching. "Looks like we're going to have a lot of fun today," Edward said, excitement in his voice. For a split second he reminded Kim of her father and that wasn't a good thing.

"I can't wait," Wynona responded, a huge smile on her face.

Kim glanced over at Duan. He reached out and took her hand in his, then leaned over and brushed a kiss across her lips. It was as if he'd read her emotions and knew she was bothered by something.

"Well, you guys," Edward announced, grabbing Wynona's hand, "I'm going to take my lady and we're heading for the Scorpion and from there to the Ferris wheel."

"See you guys later," Wynona called over her shoulder, increasing her pace to keep up with Edward.

Duan glanced over at her and tightened his hand on hers. "You okay?"

She saw concern in the depths of his eyes. "Yes, I'm fine. I just had one of those 'daddy' moments."

"Come on, let's walk," he said, keeping her hand in his. "Want to tell me about it?"

For some reason she didn't mind airing the family's dirty laundry to Duan. She'd done it before. "Fairs used to be one of my daddy's favorite places. When he took us it would be one of the few times he was normal. He would actually stay sober for a few weeks after visiting a fair. After that, it was every Friday night as usual. He would get off work and head for the nearest bar with his homies. Luckily there was always someone in the group who would bring him home later and not let him drive."

She grimaced. "It would have been better if they'd checked him in to a hotel to let him sleep it off instead of bringing him home. That would have spared Mom the beatings once he got there."

A bitter smile formed on her lips. "He would sleep late on Saturdays while I was bandaging up Mom's wounds. Then he would wake up around noon and see her bruises and become all apologetic, asking her forgiveness and telling her it wouldn't happen again. He'd become the loving husband and father, and Mom was eager to believe the best so she'd eventually forgive him. I lived to regret Fridays, Duan. Most kids in school looked forward to the weekends, but I wasn't one of them since I knew what would happen at my house."

"I'm sorry, Kim." Duan's voice was gentle. "That kind of life must have been hell to endure each week."

"It was. Because of my father I've endured a lot of hell. Forgiving doesn't come easy for me, and Mom can't seem to understand that."

"And all this time I've been the one hosting a pity party thinking the Jeffrieses were the family with all the garbage." Duane shook his head. "When my mom left, I was angry, madder than hell. I was the oldest and I had Terrence to deal with. He was a holy terror even back in the day. And then there was Olivia, who tried to take Mom's place. It's still hard to believe how a woman could leave her husband and family without looking back."

He stopped walking and so did she. He met her gaze. "I have one hell of a father, and I can't tell him enough how much I appreciate him. He had to step in and do both roles as a parent and he did it. I'm sure it wasn't easy, yet he never complained. I admire him for what he did, and I'm not sure that I could have done the same if I'd been in his place."

They began walking again and a few moments later they stopped at a vendor to buy a bag of popcorn to share. When they started walking again she asked, "Have you seen your mom since she left?"

"I didn't for a long time, almost eighteen years in fact. She left when I was twelve. A few days before my thirtieth birthday, after I'd celebrated the opening of my investigative firm, I decided to put my skills to the test and find her. I actually wanted to see her. I *needed* to see her for closure—at least I told myself it was closure. But I was hoping that when I tracked her down and she saw me, she would be remorseful, ashamed for not having the decency to pick up a phone to see how her kids were doing."

He shook his head. "But when I found her, there was no remorse or shame on her part, just annoyance at being bothered. She told me, in a not-too-nice way, that she'd gotten out of our life for a reason. She never wanted kids, wasn't the motherly type and that she didn't want to renew a relationship with any of us."

"Wow, that's deep," Kim said.

"Yes, it was. I caught a plane back to Atlanta to hear Terrence's taunting that he'd told me so. Somehow he'd known. He hadn't seen her, he hadn't wanted to see her and had been determined to move on with his life. He'd accepted her walking out on us at face value. Her betrayal, her abandonment had left its mark on the three of us, but especially on Dad."

Kim heard the bitterness in his voice. She knew it well. It was the same whenever she discussed her father with anyone. A father she hadn't seen in at least five years now. The last time had been at her paternal grandmother's funeral. He hadn't looked in the best of health and even then she guessed he was still hitting the bottle and she'd even smelled alcohol on his breath.

She glanced ahead and saw her mother and Edward. They were standing in line to get on another ride. She didn't want to think how her mother would handle it if what they suspected about Edward was true. That would definitely be a heartbreaker and her mother didn't deserve that.

Duan glanced down at her. "I know you're still worried about your mom, but you're going to have to believe that I'll do everything I can to find out the truth about Villarosas, good or bad. You're going to have to trust me."

She nodded. "I do trust you, Duan."

Kim looked away, fearful she might also admit that she had fallen in love with him.

13

DUAN EASED OUT OF BED when he heard his cell phone vibrating on the nightstand. He picked it up and quickly moved toward the bathroom. Kim was still asleep, lying naked on top of the covers. He felt his shaft get hard as he entered the bathroom. Closing the door behind him, he leaned against it as he flipped on his phone.

"Kind of late for you, isn't it, Landon?" he asked, wiping a hand down his face. It was just past midnight.

"Sorry about that. I'm still at the office."

Duan wasn't surprised. It had been that way for Landon ever since he'd lost Simone, just two days before their wedding day. She and two of her bridesmaids had shared a ride from the bachelorette party. A drunk driver had run a traffic light and the impact had been so great both vehicles had burst into flames, killing everyone involved. That had been close to four years ago and Duan knew Landon was still grieving. "I'm wondering about you not having a life, Lan."

Landon's chuckle came across the line. "Don't wonder too much, otherwise you'll sound like my mom. Anyway, I surfed the Internet and found something interesting."

"What?"

"Several old police reports, dated twenty or so years ago. They're on Villarosas. He went under the name Eduardo Villarosas then. Probably calls himself Edward for short these days."

Duan nodded. "What are the police reports about?"

"Domestic calls. Most were from neighbors complaining that he and his girlfriend were disturbing the peace with their frequent arguments. There is one where the girlfriend placed a 911 call when Villarosas threatened her because he thought she was being unfaithful."

"So there were a lot of lovers' spats."

"Seems that way. On one particular call, the girlfriend said he threatened her with bodily harm if she moved her things out of the apartment they were sharing. According to the report, she claimed Villarosas has a mean jealous streak. Police suggested she get a restraining order, which she did."

"Anything else?"

"I spoke to Chev. He's meeting with prison officials today to request time with Stein Green. Hopefully, the man will be cooperative. In the meantime, I've located a current address for Edward's old girlfriend. She still lives in the area, so I think I'll pay her a visit. I'll let you know what I find out."

From the first, Landon had assumed the disappearance of Villarosas's second wife was a hit job, a good old-fashioned murder for hire. And if that was the case, it was probably the same for Edward's first wife, as well. But without a concrete motive or a dead body, the police hadn't been able to come up with anything that would stick.

Duan couldn't wait to hear whatever Chevis could get from that guy in prison. Was he the man Mandy had met up with that day? Had he been a lover or an assassin?

"Villarosas and I are going fishing tomorrow," Duan said. "I'm going to engage him in a lot of conversation, but I don't expect him to say much. He's been pretty tight-lipped around me."

"Yeah, but there's that one chance he might lower his guard and say something meaningful."

"If I can be so lucky," Duan said.

"Well, with all of us working on this, something has to give sooner or later," Landon replied.

Duan certainly hoped it was sooner. He and Kim were supposed to leave next Sunday and he knew she had no intention of doing that without letting her mother know about their suspicions of Villarosas, proof or not.

"Let's hope so," he said.

Moments later, he ended the call and softly opened the door to walk out of the bathroom. But he paused when he immediately picked up the scent of a woman. *His woman.*

His heartbeat thundered in his chest. This was the second time he'd thought of her as his woman. But then, he would be the first to say his relationship with Kim was rather unique. What was supposed to have been a one-night stand had evolved into something a lot more. The thought of them parting ways on Sunday sent something plummeting deep in his gut. He couldn't imagine a day of not seeing her, not being with her.

He glanced across the room and saw her standing at the window. She had put on his T-shirt and had her back to him, unaware he had come out of the bathroom. That gave him a chance to just stand there and stare at her, feeling his body getting aroused in the process.

Like most men, he'd always had a pretty healthy sexual appetite, but with Kim his craving for sex was downright voracious, as insatiable as it could get. She would tempt him to no end, and the more she did, the more ravenous he became. But with her there were other things that turned him on, as well. Like the way she would lean into a kiss whenever his mouth descended on hers, and the way she would smile at him for no reason at all.

Then there was the way she would open up to him whenever she told him about her past. She had allowed him to feel the pain of her childhood, and miraculously, he had allowed her to feel the pain of his, which was something he hadn't ever done with any woman. His relationship with his mother—or his lack of one—was something he'd kept bottled up inside him. But with Kim the conversation had come easily and without any anger or feelings of guilt.

And with Kim he could have fun, like the time they'd gone fishing in the Keys on Terrence's boat, and earlier today at the fair. With a host of other folks around them, they had strolled from ride to ride, vendor to vendor, and for a few hours he had forgotten that their attachment to each other had been nothing but a show. For that period of time their relationship had seemed real.

Then there was the time when they had sat together on a bench waiting for her mother and Villarosas to get off one of the rides. He and Kim had shared a bag of cotton candy, and he'd gotten turned on watching her tongue dart out of her mouth to lick away the sticky and sweet confection from her lips. Unable to resist, he had leaned over and used his own tongue and mouth to help, and had even gone so far as to lick a bit of the sugar off her fingers. He had to stop himself from kissing her so many times today, kisses he wanted to give her for no reason at all.

Just because.

Just because he thought she was simply adorable. Just because she had to be the most sensuous woman he'd ever met. And just because everything they did was spontaneous. Especially when they made love.

"I hope there's a reason for that smile, Duan."

He hadn't noticed she'd turned around. "There is a reason, but it has nothing to do with that call I just got from Landon," he said, crossing the room to place his cell phone back on the nightstand. "The smile has everything to do with you and your behavior at the fair today."

She looked at him, surprised. "My behavior? And just what was wrong with my behavior?"

He forced his conversation with Landon to the back of his mind and crossed his arms over his chest, not bothered by the fact that he was standing in front of her totally naked and fully aroused. She was used to seeing him hard, as well as nude, since that was the way he slept every night. That was the way she slept, too, although she admitted it was something she'd only begun doing since being with him.

"I couldn't believe how many of those wild and crazy rides we went on," he said, grinning. "Most women would have backed off, claimed they were too scary. But not you. Makes me wonder just what else you like doing for kicks." Not that he didn't have a good idea. In the time they'd spent together, he had come to know her pretty well.

"I like to cook, but I wouldn't say I do it for kicks," she said, chuckling. "Mainly for survival."

Yes, he knew she liked to cook. She had awakened him that Sunday morning after their fishing trip to breakfast in bed—pan-seared pieces of the fish they'd caught, grits and the best buttermilk biscuits he'd ever eaten.

"Tell me something about you that I don't know," he suggested, moving closer to place a kiss on her nose and then her lips.

"We've already covered the good, the bad and the ugly. Besides, I can't think when you kiss me," she protested as his mouth slid to her neck.

"Do you want me to stop?" he asked, sliding his arms around her waist and proceeding to run his hands down her hips, the portion not covered by the T-shirt. He then cupped her naked backside to bring her smack against him.

"If you stop, I might have to hurt you," she threatened in a voice that sounded close to a moan. And when he returned his lips to hers, she opened her mouth to take his tongue and wrap her arms around his neck.

The scent of her aroused him even more, and he deepened the kiss while pulling her closer to him. There was this chemistry between them that had him wanting to lay his hands on her every chance he got. Even when they were just sitting together—alone or with others—he had a tendency to place his hand on her thigh, as if he liked having that connection.

From the first he'd never questioned why he liked touching her so much. He'd just accepted it, like he was doing now. He no longer had to analyze why things were the way they were between them. Why he enjoyed getting naked with her, sinking deep into her body, and reaching a climax where his release seemed endless, especially when it mingled with hers.

And why, despite the lust and desire he felt for her, he still enjoy doing simple things with her, such as sharing breakfast in bed, listening to her talk about her job at the hospital, hearing her excitement about going to med school.

He looked forward to breathing in the same air that she did, looking into her face while they ate, waking up with her scent all over him and her limbs entwined with his. Before being with her, he'd much preferred sleeping alone. Now he wondered how he would ever sleep alone again.

In an unexpected move, she withdrew her mouth from his. "Hey, Jeffries, you're slow. You're already naked, so what's the holdup with me?" She took a step back and whipped the T-shirt over her head, tossing it aside. "Don't you like to see me without clothes anymore?"

If only she knew. "I always enjoy seeing you without clothes, Kim," he said, reaching out and bringing her naked body back to him. And that was no lie. There wasn't a part of her body that he didn't like looking at, touching or tasting.

"Then I can't have you losing your touch," she said, rubbing against him. His erection got harder when it came into contact with her wet heat.

"I'll never lose my touch when it comes to you, beautiful," he said, sweeping her off her feet and into his arms. He headed toward the bed. The primitive male in him wanted her with a need that was consuming every part of his body, sending heat rumbling in his belly.

She kissed his nose and lips. "I love a confident man."

When she slid out of his arms onto the bed, he ran his hands all over her, needing to touch her everywhere. A degree of hot energy surged in his groin, and when she propped herself on a pillow in that position he loved so much, he leaned down and with the tip of his finger traced a path down her throat and chest, pausing when he got to her stomach.

He drew circles around her navel while thinking about the child she'd said she wanted one day, and wondered about the man who would eventually plant his seed inside her to make it happen. He inhaled sharply when the mere thought of such a thing—Kim having another man's baby—snatched his breath away.

Fighting back a crazy impulse that was running through his mind, he removed his hand from her to retrieve a condom from the nightstand. How many of these had they gone through already? Hell, he wasn't counting and he figured neither was she. The main thing was that they were acting as responsible adults and using them.

He sheathed his penis in the condom, and when he glanced over at Kim, the eyes watching him were filled with hot desire. He had come to recognize that look—an urgent and silent message that told him how desperate she was for him to get inside her. That thought sent what felt like liquid fire rushing through his veins.

"You like torturing me, don't you, Duan?"

"No more than you like torturing me—the way you're doing now, lying there with your legs spread open. Whenever I see you that way all I can think about is getting inside you." But it was more than that. He craved her like a man who craved a woman who was in his blood. His head reeled at the very thought.

He watched as she took her hand and slid it down to her thigh, then back up to splay it across her stomach, the same stomach he'd gazed at moments ago. Then she shifted her body to spread her legs even wider, giving him a pure, unadulterated visual of what lay between them. His erection stirred at the same time his heart did.

Unable to resist any longer, he moved toward the bed. "I want you, Kim."

"Prove it."

She tossed the words out the moment he placed one knee on the bed and reached for her. "Come here," he said, lifting her off the bed into his arms and toward his waiting and hungry mouth. And then he tumbled on his back with her on top of him, their mouths still locked.

Kim gripped Duan's shoulders and concentrated on kissing him with the same intensity that he was kissing her, with a hunger that was sending hot blood racing through her veins. Their mouths fitted together perfectly, like those Lego blocks she had as a kid, and they mated with a fervor that was unrelenting.

He raked his fingers through the curls on her head and she gripped his shoulders tightly as their tongues dueled and tangled, sucked and licked while something fierce and potent tugged deep inside her.

She tried to focus on his mouth and not on what she was feeling in her heart. This wasn't just sex for her. This was love in a way she'd never thought possible.

She pulled her mouth away and released a moan from deep within her throat, staring down at him. The look in his eyes was as hot and as predatory as anything she'd ever seen. And behind those dark pupils she sensed a need, the magnitude of which had her inner muscles gripping and tensing something awful.

She moved her hands from his shoulders and took hold of his wrists, placing them on both sides of his head to make him her prisoner, not of war but of love. She could feel her love in every inch of him, in everything about him.

Holding his hands in her tight grip, she widened her legs and lowered her body toward his erection, angling herself in such a way that allowed for deeper penetration. She began easing down slowly and watched in heated fascination as his erection slid between the folds of her sex until she had taken in his entire length.

She heard the hitch in his breath and saw his jaw tighten. The hands she was gripping felt hot and his solid thickness stretched her, bathing her in sensations until she was shuddering almost uncontrollably.

He stared up at her and she lost herself in the depths of his gaze. He was so powerfully male and she quivered at the thought of him being embedded so deep inside her. It was as if she could feel him touching her womb, and the realization stroked her heart.

The moment she released his hands, he automatically reached out and gripped her hips, lifting his own off the bed to thrust even deeper into her. Then he pulled back and plunged into her again.

"Ride me, Kim."

The plea, spoken in a guttural groan, unraveled her senses, fragmented her control, and she—who'd never ridden a horse in her life—began imitating what she'd seen on television. Clutching his sides with her knees as if she was riding bareback, she established a steady rhythm, moving up and down his shaft as he penetrated her more deeply.

She continued to ride him, building her confidence, flexing her inner muscles to squeeze everything out of him. When he lifted his head off the pillow to suck on her shoulder and then capture a nipple with his mouth, it seemed that every single thing inside her exploded.

She threw her head back as she continued to ride him, needing to possess him that way, needing him to surrender everything to her and knowing the moment he did. And the thought that he did set her on fire.

His hips rose off the bed as he let out a guttural groan and thrust into her. His hands locked around her hips and she felt him come inside her and knew at that moment that the condom had broken. The heat of his semen was filling her core and plunging her into one earth-shattering orgasm. She opened her eyes and met his gaze and knew he was aware of what had happened but had no intention of stopping now.

He clenched his jaw and thrust deep inside her once more as he came yet again. The air surrounding them was filled with the thick aroma of sex, but the only thing Kim could focus on was all the pleasure he was giving her. She gripped his shoulders more firmly as sensation upon sensation washed over her, through her.

Moments later, she slumped down on him, unable to move after what had to be the most intense mating session any one woman could endure.

"Kim?"

She heard him whisper her name and was fully aware of his concern. She lifted her head slightly and met his gaze. She knew what he was about to say. "It's okay. I'm on the Pill."

"Oh."

Was that disappointment she heard in his voice? Part of her knew it couldn't be, but another part wished that it were. They held each other's gaze for a long moment, and then his arms closed around her. Without disengaging their bodies, he snuggled her closer into his arms, kissed her so tenderly it almost brought tears to her eyes. Then she rested her head in the cradle of his shoulder.

She closed her eyes and knew if she never made love to another man again, this would be enough.

14

"DID LANDON HAVE any updates?"

The bedcovers rustled as Kim shifted position to ease off him. Duan lay on his side to face her, missing the feel of her warm body on top of his. He'd hoped she had forgotten about Landon's midnight call.

He glanced down and saw the damage done to the condom. They weren't cheap, which presented proof of the intensity of their lovemaking. He needed to go into the bathroom, but first he would answer her, not sure how much he would tell her. Already the thought of her mother spending any time with Villarosas bothered her. If he were to level with Kim that he had reason to believe the man had a jealous streak, there was no telling what she might say or do.

But still, he knew he had to tell her. She deserved to know. She had every right to know. "Landon spent most of the day surfing the Net and got some information on Villarosas that he figured we should know."

She lifted a brow. "What kind of information?"

"About twenty years ago, Villarosas and his girlfriend at the time had had a number of disorderly peace citations when their arguments got out of hand."

"And?"

Of course she'd know there was more, Duan thought. "And according to the woman, he has a tendency to display a jealous streak on occasion."

Concern flashed in her eyes and she made a move to get off the bed, but he quickly reached out and grabbed her wrist. "Hey, that's the woman's side of things. Her accusations. No charges were ever filed against Villarosas and he never physically touched the woman. They just caused a lot of ruckus that got on their neighbors' nerves. Who knows, the girlfriend might have given him a reason to be jealous. Some women do that sort of thing to get their man's attention."

It took a while for what he'd said to sink in and then she asked, "And you're sure there were no charges of any type of abuse?"

He nodded. "Positive."

She seemed to relax somewhat and he released her wrist. "My mother is probably the last person I should worry about when it comes to physical abuse. She swore my father was the last man who would ever touch her that way. While I was in college she and some of the ladies in the apartment complex where she was living got together and arranged for one of the police officers who patrolled the area to teach a self-defense class. She enjoyed it so much that when the class was over she took additional lessons at the junior college."

He nodded, impressed. "How good is she?"

Kim shrugged. "She's not a black belt, but she has a yellow belt."

"Some women don't have that."

She smiled faintly. "I know, including me. While Mom was taking those classes, I was motivated to do the same, but I was away at college and studying all the time. Then later, my excuse was the long hours I was working at the hospital."

Duan glanced over at the clock as he eased out of bed. It was past two in the morning. "I need to go into the bathroom to take care of this," he said. "I'm sorry this happened, Kim. It's a first for me, but I assure you I'm in good health. I take that seriously."

She waved off his words. "No sweat, and rest assured that I'm in good health, as well. It was an accident. I don't want you to lose sleep over it because I won't. Like I told you, I'm on the Pill so I'm good."

Duan nodded. He figured hearing that again should make him feel a whole lot better, but it didn't. He turned and headed toward the bathroom thinking it would not have bothered him in the least if she hadn't been on the Pill.

He pulled in a shaky breath, knowing why he felt that way. He had fallen in love with her.

KIM SAT AT THE TABLE in her mother's kitchen and sipped her hot chocolate. Duan and Edward had left hours ago to go fishing and her mother was busy baking a cake for a sick member of the church. She was glad her mother was back to baking again. Spending time in the kitchen had always been one of Wynona's favorite pastimes.

Three consecutive knocks sounded at the back door. "Come on in, Bennie—it's open," her mother called out.

When Mr. Bennie walked in, Kim immediately remembered what Duan had said a few days ago about the man having a thing for her mom. "Good morning, Mr. Bennie," she greeted him.

He looked over in her direction and returned her smile. "Hey there, Sunshine," he said, calling her by the name he'd given her years ago when she was a toddler. She was Sunshine and his daughter Valerie had been Sweet Pea. "Are you doing okay this morning?"

"Yes, sir, I'm fine. What do you have there?" she asked as he placed a huge basket on the kitchen counter.

"Vegetables for your mom from my garden," he said proudly. "Sweet potatoes, squash, tomatoes and okra. I always share with Nona."

"That's nice," Kim said, closely watching the interaction between the two.

Her mother had crossed the room to check out the basket, and Mr. Bennie said something to make her laugh. But he'd always made her mother laugh. They were old friends and enjoyed each other's company, which was why Kim had never paid them any attention before.

And she had never paid any attention to the fact that Mr. Bennie was rather nice-looking. Tall, with dark hair, gray eyes and a roasted-almond skin tone. It was quite obvious that he had kept himself in good physical shape for a fifty-seven-year-old man. For years he'd owned a hardware supply store in town but had sold it not long after Valerie graduated from college.

Wynona crossed the room to open the refrigerator and Kim watched as Mr. Bennie's gaze followed her mother's every step. And then, as if he remembered she was in the kitchen, he glanced over at Kim and gave her a nervous smile, knowing he'd been caught ogling her mother.

He cleared his throat. "So, Sunshine, how long will you be in town?"

"Just until the weekend. I'm flying back out on Sunday," she said, hoping that was true. She was thinking about contacting the hospital for extended time if she needed to do so.

Her mother returned to the counter with the eggs for the cake. "Kim came home to meet Edward," Wynona said, smiling. "She was afraid we would marry before she had a chance to do that. Now she's talked to me about putting off the wedding until next month, when she could get more time off work. Of course Edward will have to agree to it."

Mr. Bennie nodded, and Kim could tell that Wynona's wedding to Edward was not something he wanted to talk about. "I called Sweet Pea last night and told her all about you making medical school," he said, as if he needed to change the subject. "She told me to tell you congratulations and that she knows one day you'll make a fine doctor."

Kim smiled. "Thanks."

"And just so you know, Sunshine, I like your young man. He's nice."

Flutters kicked in Kim's stomach. If only Duan was really hers. "Thanks again."

Mr. Bennie rubbed his hands down his jeans. "Well, I'd better be getting back next door. I need to check in on my computer to see if any orders came in this morning." Kim knew he had an online business that specialized in selling figurines. Customers placed orders through the Internet and he sent them to the factory where the merchandise was kept. That way he didn't have to worry about inventory. "I hope to see you again before you leave, Sunshine," he said.

Kim nodded. "And I hope to see you, as well. In fact I'm going to make a point of stopping by and saying goodbye. You have a nice day, Mr. Bennie."

"You do the same, Sunshine." He smiled at her mother. "I'll talk to you later, Nona."

When the door closed behind him, Kim knew Duan was right. Although her mother was clueless, Mr. Bennie was sweet on her.

"HEY, YOU'RE NOT a bad fisherman," Edward said, smiling over at Duan.

Duan forced a smile back. "Thanks. I try to get out on the water as often as I can. It relaxes me."

"Same here. Do you own a boat?"

Duan shook his head. "No, but my brother has a beauty of one in the Keys. He lets me use it whenever I want, and I fly down there every chance I get."

Edward nodded. "And that's how you met Kim?"

Duan remembered Kim had told the story of how they met to both Edward and Wynona and wondered if perhaps the man was trying to compare their versions. "Yes. Her best friend Sherri is married to my brother Terrence."

Edward grinned. "That's right, the *Holy Terror*. I used to keep up with him when he was playing pro with the Miami Dolphins. I hated when he called it quits."

"A number of people did, but it was his decision to make. Terrence had played football since he was in grade school and always said he only wanted to play until he was thirty. He didn't want an injury to take him out. I agreed with and respected his decision."

"So are you and Kim thinking of having kids?"

Duan nearly dropped his fishing rod, wondering where that question had come from. "Probably one day.

Kim has plans to go to medical school." Again he was aware that Edward knew that. Was this another verification question?

"Wynona is hoping Kim can squeeze in marriage and a baby before she becomes a doctor," Edward said, casting out his rod.

Duan shrugged. "It's whatever Kim wants," he said. "The beauty of our relationship is that we're in agreement on just about everything."

"And I guess you trust her completely."

The statement sounded sarcastic. "Yes, I trust her completely. Just like I'm sure you trust Wynona completely."

Edward nodded. "Oh, yeah. Sure. I trust Wynona. I wouldn't be marrying her if I didn't."

Duan studied the man for a second. "I guess you wouldn't since this will be your *third* marriage, right?"

The beer bottle Edward had been holding nearly slipped from his grasp and he quickly glanced over at Duan. "Yes, it will be my third marriage."

"Hey, you know what they say. Three's a charm."

Duan wasn't sure whether Edward's smile was genuine. "Yes, you're right," Edward said. "Three's a charm."

LATER THAT NIGHT, Duan got a call from Chevis. "I was able to convince the warden of my need to talk to Green and he agreed. Our meeting is set for Wednesday at noon. Has anyone heard from Tron?"

"Landon spoke with him a few days ago," Duan said of the former FBI agent turned private investigator, Antron Blair. "He's checking out Edward's cell phone records from five years ago and his land phone records from ten years ago, as well as his bank statements for the same period. I hope to hear something from him soon."

He shoved off the bed when Kim walked out of the bathroom. Wynona had gone to Bible study at church, and instead of accepting her invitation to join her, he and Kim had decided to go to a movie at the multiplex around the corner from the hotel. He usually would not have wasted his time or money on the flick, but he would suffer through it for her.

"All right, Chevis, keep me informed on how things turn out with your meeting with Stein Green on Wednesday."

After flipping off the phone, he gave Kim his total attention. There was no hope for it. She was wearing a hot pink tank top and a short black skirt that showed what good-looking legs she had. He'd much prefer staying in the hotel room tonight and messing around with her, but he knew she had her heart set on seeing this movie. Still…

He crossed the room when he saw the trouble she was having putting her necklace on. He came to stand behind her. "Need help?"

She glanced over her shoulder at him. "Yes, thanks."

He pushed her curls aside to have access to her neck. She smelled so good. But then, she always did.

"You were right, Duan."

"About what?"

"Mr. Bennie having a thing for Mom. I can't believe I've never noticed it before."

He finished with the necklace and leaned down to place a kiss on her neck at the same time she brushed her backside against his crotch. He sucked in a deep breath at the contact. Damn, it felt good. "I hate to say that I told you so," he said, wrapping his arms around her middle to bring her even closer to him.

"You know what I wish," she said, shifting to look over her shoulder at him.

He leaned in and brushed a kiss across her lips. "No, what do you wish?"

"That Mom would notice, too. But they've been friends for so long she probably doesn't see him as anything other than a friend."

"I can believe that." Duan went back to her neck, sucking in his favorite spot, not caring that a passion mark would probably be visible tomorrow. "Dad didn't start noticing Cathy until she turned up the heat."

"How did she do that?"

Duan chuckled. "Hell if I know, but I'm sure Olivia does. Terrence and I figured the less we knew, the better. All we do know is that they went to New York on a business trip together and things changed for them after that."

He sucked in another deep breath when Kim intentionally wiggled her backside against his crotch again. "Hey, I wouldn't do that too many times if I were you," he warned.

She laughed when he took a step back. "Whatever," she said, turning around to him. "Ready to go?"

"I guess."

She lifted a brow. "You don't sound too anxious."

He smiled. "Well, I'd rather see a lot of blood and guts instead of a lot of kissy, kissy, bed, bed."

She threw her head back and laughed, and the way the curls on her head went flying around her face sent sensations all through his gut. He thought at that moment she was simply beautiful.

Taking his hand, she pulled him toward the door. "We'll see a blood and guts movie the next time. I promise."

Duan allowed himself to be dragged out of the room. He hoped she remembered the promise she'd just made because he intended for her to keep it.

15

KIM TRIED TO KEEP BUSY while Duan talked on the phone. The call had come early Thursday morning, waking them up at seven. At first she'd thought he was talking to Landon, but after a while it became obvious a conference call was taking place and he was conversing with several people. She had showered and had taken care of her hair but he was still on the phone.

The expression on his face looked serious. She tried to remain calm and not jump to any conclusions. To kill time, she walked around the room, tidying up a little bit. Although the hotel had someone to come in and clean their room every day, there was no need for the person to think they were slobs. Although she would have to admit the only untidy spot was the bed.

Bedcovers were strewn all over the floor, the sheets were all twisted and a couple of pillows were at the foot of the bed. She didn't have to figure out how that happened. Last night she and Duan had tried several new positions, and one required her at one end of the bed with him at the other, their heads buried between each other's thighs. Talk about a fantasy come true. Pleasure stirred her insides just remembering it.

She turned toward him when she heard his phone flip shut and met his gaze. Immediately, she knew—for better or for worse—that he'd found out something. She inhaled deeply to prepare herself for whatever he had to say.

"Come here, Kim," he said in that deep, throaty voice she loved so much.

She crossed the room to the wingback chair where he sat and he reached out and pulled her down into his lap. She turned to him. "Yes?"

"That was everyone," he said, draping his hands across her thighs.

"Everyone?" she asked. "All four of them?"

"Yes, Landon, Antron, Brett and Chevis. We had a conference call since there were several updates."

She nodded. "So what did they find out?"

When Duan hesitated she knew he was looking for the right words. "Go ahead, Duan. Tell me. Is my mother in any danger?"

Instead of answering her, he said, "Landon went to talk to Villarosas's old girlfriend and she backed up her claim of over twenty years ago. She said Villarosas has a nasty jealous streak and that he'd threatened to get rid of her several times when he thought she was unfaithful to him. She claims she wasn't, but had gotten sick and tired of him making false allegations and threats that she believed he would carry out, so she split."

Kim nodded. "But that was over twenty-some years ago. Right?"

"Right. Now, Chevis went to a prison in Florida yesterday to visit Stein Green. After some intense questioning—relentless interrogation Chevis-style—Green admitted that Edward Villarosas hired him to get rid of both of his wives because they were unfaithful."

Kim leaped out of Duan's lap. "And that bastard thinks he's going to marry my mother?" she said in a raised voice.

"Kim, calm down."

"Have the police been notified? When will he be arrested? When is—"

"Kim, please let me finish," he interrupted, standing up as well. "What we have is an allegation from a convicted killer, a man already serving a life sentence with no chance of parole for armed robbery where a police officer was gunned down. All he's done is verify what we suspected all along, especially with Villarosas's ironclad alibis. But we need more than just the word of a criminal. We need concrete proof and we're working with Green to get that. No court of law will bring charges against Villarosas based on Green's word."

"What kind of proof is needed?"

"Finding their bodies would be nice."

Kim's hands flew to her mouth and Duan knew she was remembering the two women. "Oh, my God, Duan, something has to be done. My heart goes out to their families."

"And something will be done to the fullest extent of the law. But we don't have enough to uphold a conviction. Right now, all we have is a criminal's word. Until we have evidence to substantiate his claim, there's nothing we can do. But rest assured, we're getting that evidence."

"How?"

"From Villarosas's old bank accounts, we can show that large amounts of money were withdrawn during the times Green claims he was paid."

"That's not enough proof?"

"No. We've also obtained old phone call records between Green and Villarosas, but again, that doesn't prove anything since there are no recorded conversations. It will be Green's word against Villarosas's, and who do you think a jury would believe? A man already in jail for life or a man who appears to be a model citizen? Those incidents with Villarosas's girlfriend over twenty years ago would not be admissible."

"So what's going to be done?"

"As we speak, a team of both local and federal officers are searching a wooded area near Orlando and another in Atlanta where Green said the remains are. Regardless, Villarosas will be picked up and brought in for questioning today. Detectives from the Atlanta police department are already on their way here for that. If those remains are located, Villarosas will be charged immediately and extradited back to Georgia."

Duan sighed deeply and rubbed a hand over the top of his head. "What we need to do now is talk to your mother. Villarosas is going to be questioned and it's best she finds out from us. I will also need to come clean with her and tell her my role in all of this."

Kim nodded. "I agree, and we should tell her in person. She isn't expecting Edward to come over until later since this is the day he plays golf. So hopefully we can talk to her alone. Mom is going to be crushed."

"Yes, but when the evidence is laid out before her, I'm sure she'll agree that these are serious charges and those allegations being made are—"

Duan's cell phone went off. "Excuse me." He flipped it on. "Yes, Landon?" He nodded a few times. "Yes, okay, and thanks for letting us know."

He flipped off the phone and met Kim's gaze. "That was Landon. He wanted to let me know remains were found exactly where Green said they would be, and the authorities are working to obtain positive IDs. If they are Villarosas's missing wives, then it's safe to say he'll be booked and extradited back to Atlanta to face murder charges."

Kim was already grabbing her purse off the bed. "I need to get to Mom and tell her."

Duan was already moving toward the door. "Come on, let's go."

"I STILL CAN'T REACH Mom," Kim said, putting her cell phone back in her purse. She glanced over at Duan as he drove the rental car out of the hotel parking lot. "I want to at least let her know we're on our way over there so she won't go anywhere. She visits Aunt Gert on occasion."

"It's a nice day so she might be out in the yard."

"Yes," Kim said, smiling. "She loves her flower garden."

She was trying to think of positive things, but it was hard to do so knowing how close her mother had come to marrying Edward. The thought that the man had arranged for his two wives to be killed sent chills down her body. She dreaded telling her mother, but at least all this was coming to an end before her mom could become his next victim.

"Thanks for all the hard work you and your friends did. Just think of how long Villarosas has gotten away with this. With Green already in jail for an unrelated crime, he probably thought he was home free."

"That's a good assumption to make. The man evidently has mental issues, and I won't be satisfied until he's behind bars where he belongs."

Kim nodded. "I'm surprised Stein Green decided to talk."

"He had nothing to lose since he's already doing life with no chance of parole. He probably feels good about squealing on Villarosas since he's in prison and Villarosas is still out enjoying freedom." Duan pulled to a stop at the red light.

"In that case, why didn't he speak up sooner?"

"Green probably figured no one was going to take him seriously, but since Chevis came around asking, he was more than ready to spill his guts. According to Chevis, the man was full of information and didn't hesitate in telling them where the women's bodies were."

"And he admitted to killing them?"

"Yes, after beating them up first. Hc claimed those were Villarosas's instructions to teach his cheating wives a lesson."

Kim shuddered at the thought and was glad when Duan pulled into her mother's driveway. She had unsnapped her seat belt and was out of the car as soon as it came to a complete stop. She began racing toward the front door.

"She's not at home, Sunshine."

Kim stopped walking so fast that she almost missed the step to the door. Duan's arm reached out to steady her.

She glanced across the yard at Mr. Bennie, who was working in his flower garden. "She's not here? Do you know if she went to visit Aunt Gert?"

He shook his head as he took off his work gloves. "No, she left early this morning with Edward Villarosas. She had an overnight bag so I assume they've gone out of town."

"What! Oh, my God, I hope you're wrong about that, Mr. Bennie." Kim frantically fished through her purse for her mother's door key, spilling most of the contents on the ground.

"I'll get the door," Duan said, bending down to retrieve the items that had fallen from her purse, including the keys. With his arms planted firmly around Kim's waist, he slid the key in the door and pushed it open. She rushed past him and was inside before he could draw his next breath.

A piece of paper was sitting on the dining-room table and she quickly raced over to pick it up. When she finished reading it, she turned to Duan, her eyes filled with anger. "The bastard talked Mom into eloping to Vegas," she said heatedly, letting the paper fall from her hand onto the floor. "She can't marry him! She can't!"

Duan crossed the room and pulled her into his arms. "No, she can't, and if we have to contact every wedding chapel in Vegas to make sure that she doesn't then—"

"Excuse me, I don't mean to intrude, but is everything all right?"

Duan and Kim glanced over to see Mr. Bennie standing in the doorway. Kim pulled out of Duan's arms and rushed over to him. "Mr. Bennie, when you saw Mom this morning, did she look okay? Did it appear as if she was being forced to leave or anything like that?"

The man's eyebrows shot up, as if surprised by Kim's line of questioning. "No, she seemed to be leaving of her own free will and was in a good mood, as always. She smiled and waved when she saw me. I was putting out the garbage. That was around seven this morning."

Kim nodded. She found some comfort in knowing Edward hadn't killed the other two women himself, which meant her mother was probably not in any immediate danger. But still, the thought of Wynona traveling alone with the man was unsettling.

"What is it, Sunshine? What's wrong?"

Duan walked over to them. "If you don't mind coming inside, Mr. Bennie, we can explain things."

"All right."

Duan closed the door behind the man and pulled Kim close to his side. She was shivering in both fear and anger.

"Mr. Jeffries, I know you might think it's none of my business, but if there's something wrong, please tell me. Nona and I are very good friends. I care about her deeply."

"I know you do, Mr. Bennie," he said truthfully. "And she's going to need you a lot when this is all over."

The man glanced over at Kim in concern. "I'll always be there for her. Now please tell me what's going on."

Duan inhaled deeply. "Edward Villarosas is wanted for questioning by the police."

Mr. Bennie looked surprised. "The police? What for?"

Duan's arms tightened around Kim's waist. "For arranging the deaths of his two wives."

16

KIM WAS PACING the floor and so was Mr. Bennie. They both had worried looks on their faces. Kim had tried a number of times to reach her mother by phone but was unsuccessful.

Duan had contacted the Shreveport police and then placed a call to the airlines to check flights for Vegas. He'd been able to find out Wynona and Edward's flight number, and according to the airline, the flight had landed in Vegas over an hour ago. So why wasn't Wynona answering her phone?

The Vegas police had been contacted and a warrant had been issued for Villarosas's arrest. The one good thing was that Wynona wasn't taken by force, which meant she still didn't know the type of man Villarosas really was. Duan was of the opinion that Villarosas had no reason to harm Wynona since he probably felt secure in their relationship. At least for now.

He looked over at Kim and she gave him a faint smile. A part of him realized why he loved her so much. She cared about her family. She was loyal. And she was nothing like the woman his father had married, who had deserted her husband and children. Kim was all goodness. All caring. And she wanted children.

He understood why he enjoyed sleeping so close to her at night, their bodies touching, and then awakening beside her every morning for playtime. He enjoyed seeing her eat, swallow, lick cotton candy from her lips. He had enjoyed their late-night talks where he would sit with her in his lap for hours. He even enjoyed sitting next to her at the movies, sharing buttered popcorn with her. And although the movie wasn't anything he'd wanted to see, it hadn't mattered as long as she was there beside him. Just hearing her chuckle through a couple of scenes had been music to his ears.

He had fallen in love with a woman who didn't have room for him in her future.

He knew all about her plans. Four years in medical school. What right did he have to ask her to do anything differently now that he knew he loved? And why would she even consider such a thing? Although he had fallen in love with her, that didn't mean she had fallen in love with him. As far as he knew, and as she'd reminded him several times, she had no intentions of having a serious relationship with a man, and what he was considering was a serious as it could get.

She deserved to have her dream and he wouldn't rob her of it like her father had done when he'd taken that money. This was her chance to do the one thing she'd always wanted to do, and he loved her too much to stand in her way. So he would stick to his original plan.

When all this was over, he would leave for Atlanta. But he intended to keep up with what she was doing through Sherri, because no matter where Kim went or what she did, she would always unknowingly have his heart.

Duan was pulled from the depths of his thoughts as a car door slammed. He glanced out the window and saw an unmarked patrol car pull into the yard, then watched as three men got out. He recognized one of them as Landon. He assumed one man was a detective from the Atlanta police department who'd come to question Villarosas, and the other was a detective from Shreveport.

Kim heard the car, as well, and she quickly moved toward the front door, holding her breath with every step she took. And she didn't have to glance over her shoulder to know Duan was right behind her.

She looked into the faces of the three men. "Yes, may I help you?"

"Ms. Cannon?"

"Yes."

One of the men flashed a badge in front of her. "I'm Detective Mark Hogan of the Shreveport police department, this is Detective Arnold Reddick with the Atlanta police department, and Landon Chestnut from the Peachtree Private Investigative Firm."

Kim's gaze swept by the two men and went straight to Landon. Duan had mentioned he would be accompanying the detective coming from Atlanta.

After shaking hands with the men, she said, "Yes, please come in."

Introductions were made to Duan and Mr. Bennie. She watched the easy comraderie between Duan and Landon, indicating the long friendship between the two. Landon, who seemed to be a couple of years younger than Duan, was a very handsome man. But in her opinion no man was more handsome than Duan.

"Have you heard anything?" Kim asked anxiously.

Detective Hogan glanced over at her. "The police department in Vegas has been notified and they're checking the registry of all the hotels. There's quite a number of them. A current photograph of your mother and Villarosas was wired to Vegas and everyone is on the lookout for them. We've also alerted several popular chapels."

At that moment Kim's cell phone rang and she raced across the room to pick it up from the table, not recognizing the phone number. "Yes?"

"Kim?"

"Mom!" she nearly screamed with both relief and excitement. Everyone raced across the room to her.

"Mom! Where are you? I've been trying to reach you and—"

"Kim, sweetheart, please listen. I had to call you. Edward is acting weird and accusing me of all sorts of stuff. I'm in Las Vegas, and on the way from the airport to our hotel I convinced him that I needed to use the bathroom and couldn't wait. So we stopped at one of those fast-food restaurants. I'm using this woman's phone that I met here in the ladies' room. The battery in my phone died so I couldn't call you, and when I asked Edward about using his phone he accused me of wanting to call Bennie."

"Mr. Bennie?" Kim asked, glancing over at the neighbor, who stared back at her with a curious look on his face.

"Yes. Edward dropped by unexpectedly last night while Bennie was there. I don't know what's got into him. He was fine until we got to Vegas and then he began yelling and accusing me of all sorts of things, especially having an affair with Bennie."

Kim struggled to stay calm. "Mom, listen, don't go back out to Edward's car. Use the lady's phone and call 911 and tell them exactly where you are."

"Kim, it's not that serious. Edward just needs time to think about what he's saying and—"

"Mom, please do what I ask. Edward is wanted by the police." Kim hadn't wanted to break the news to her mother this way, but she didn't have a choice.

"Wanted by the police? Kim, that is utter non-sense."

"No it's not, Mom. The police detective is here and needs to talk to you. Please listen to what he says and tell them where you are."

Kim handed Detective Hogan her cell phone and then moved aside to inform Duan, Mr. Bennie and Landon of what her mother had said. Detective Reddick was talking on his cell, contacting the police in Vegas, letting them know of her mother's phone call.

"Edward began acting strange," Kim said. "And he accused Mom of having an affair with you, Mr. Bennie. Mom said Edward got that idea when he dropped by last night and you and Mom were together."

Mr. Bennie nodded. "Yes, I was here last night. Nona and I were shelling peas."

"Well, evidently Edward got upset, which is probably what prompted him to convince her to fly off to Vegas with him."

"Why didn't she contact you on her cell phone?" Duan asked.

"Her battery died. And according to her, Edward wouldn't let her use his phone, so she pretended she had to go to the ladies' room, which got him to make a stop. She called from the ladies' room of a fast-food restaurant using another woman's phone. That's where she is now."

Kim glanced over at the two detectives. Hogan was still talking to her mother and she eased closer to hear what was being said.

"Yes, Ms. Cannon. He needs to be brought in for the murder of his two wives." He paused and then said, "Yes, ma'am, murder. I know this comes as a shock, but it's true. His hired killer told us where to find the bodies. We've contacted the Vegas law enforcement as to where you are and they're on their way."

Hogan nodded. "Yes, I would advise you to keep the bathroom door locked until they get there." He nodded again. "Good thinking. Yes, please hold for a minute."

Hogan then relayed to the others what was happening. "The lady whose phone she's using has agreed to stay with her and they've locked themselves in the restroom. Edward has knocked on the door twice, but Ms. Cannon has kept him at bay by saying she had a little emergency and needed more time."

"The Vegas police are a couple of blocks away," Reddick said, before returning to his own call.

Hogan conveyed that information to Wynona. He nodded at whatever she was saying and then replied, "Yes, ma'am, you're right. People are not always what they seem to be."

Kim swallowed, wondering how her mother was going to feel when she found out that Duan had been an imposter, as well.

"The police are there now?" Hogan glanced over at Reddick, who nodded to confirm. "Yes, then it's safe to unlock the bathroom door and yes, everything is going to be all right, Ms. Cannon. You did a smart thing getting away from Villarosas." He nodded again. "Yes, she's right here."

Hogan glanced over at Kim. "Your mother would like to speak with you."

Kim quickly moved forward to take the phone. "Yes, Mom, I'm glad it's over and that you're all right." She actually felt her heart ache for her mother, especially when she heard the sobs in her mother's voice.

Her eyes began getting teary, and Duan came forward and pulled her closer to his side when she said, "Yes, Mom, we want you to come home, too."

FOUR HOURS LATER, Wynona was back home. Kim had hoped the family would not get wind of what had happened for a while, but when Edward's arrest made the evening news everyone began calling.

Kim thought her mother a real trouper after enduring questioning by the Vegas, Shreveport and Atlanta police departments. Edward had been transported from Vegas straight to Atlanta. Wynona said he'd asked to see her and she had agreed, although it had been hard. He hadn't denied the charges and instead had tried to get her to see why his wives deserved to die. Basically, he'd ended up confessing his crimes to her and the Vegas detectives.

Wynona returned to Shreveport on a law enforcement plane, had been given a sedative and was now resting comfortably. Kim had managed to keep the family members away and for once appreciated that they understood her mother's need to rest.

She sat in the chair beside the bed watching her mother sleep. She had contacted the hospital to ask for an additional week off, knowing she would need to stay with her mother to help her through this traumatic episode.

She sighed. Wynona deserved a man to love, respect and cherish her. After Edward's actions, she wondered if her mother would finally realize that you couldn't seek your happiness in others—it had to first come from within.

That lesson was something that she herself would have to accept in the coming days. No matter what, she couldn't let despair take hold of her at the thought that pretty soon she and Duan would be parting ways.

Once her mother woke up and they had a chance to talk, she would tell Wynona everything, including the fact that Duan was not her fiancé and that his sole purpose in being in Shreveport was to prove or disprove Edward's guilt.

Duan and his associates had worked hard to do just that. And now with the two cases finally closed, there was nothing to keep him in Shreveport. She wondered if he planned to fly out with Landon first thing in the morning.

Kim fought back her tears, thinking no one had asked her to fall in love with Duan. Their relationship was never meant to be long-term. She had known that, yet she had allowed her heart to get involved in what should have been nothing more than red-hot sex. She could only blame herself for the outcome.

A warm pair of lips touched the side of her face and she didn't have to look up to know that Duan was there. And then she felt strong arms lift her up and carry her out of the room.

She knew she had to pull herself together and not think of the man she was losing, since he'd never been hers anyway.

"I know you wanted to watch over your mother, but you don't need to sleep in that chair, Kim," Duan whispered against her forehead.

"And just where are you taking me?" she asked, cuddling deeper into his arms, knowing this would probably be the last time she would have a chance to do so.

"To one of the guest bedrooms. Then I'm leaving to go pack up our things at the hotel. I figure you'll want to be close to your mom for a while, especially tonight. I'll be flying out with Landon to Atlanta first thing in the morning to provide what information I have for the women's families."

Kim tried to keep her heart from breaking but it shattered into little pieces anyway. He wasn't wasting any time putting distance between them. "I can go back to the hotel with you to help you pack things up and—"

"No, you need to stay here with your mom. She needs you."

And I need you, she wanted to scream, but fought the urge to do so. More than anything she wanted to make love with him one final time, to release him from her heart and soul.

"Where is Landon?" she asked when she felt him gently place her on the bed.

"He left to go over to police headquarters and file our reports." He stretched out beside her on the bed, pulling her into his arms.

"Are you hungry, Kim? I prepared a pot of soup for you and your mom."

She shook her head as she settled her body against his. "Thanks, but I'm not hungry. Is Mr. Bennie still here?"

"No, he left, but I have a feeling he'll be back. It wouldn't surprise me if he makes his feelings for your mother known to her. He admitted to me that he's been in love with her for a long time. At least three years now, but he was afraid to make his move, afraid she would turn him down as a suitor and then he would lose her as a friend."

Kim hoped Mr. Bennie did let her mother know of his feelings. Wynona would need time to heal from Edward's betrayal, but Kim was sure Mr. Bennie would give her all the time she needed.

"Kim?"

She looked up at Duan. "Yes?"

"Everything worked out, didn't it?"

She nodded. "Yes, and I have you and your friends to thank for that. I don't want to think about what could have happened if you hadn't remembered Edward's name. What if Mom had married him? He was a time bomb just waiting to go off. The man truly has a mental problem and I hope he gets the treatment he needs."

"At least he's out of your mother's life, and with the love of you, her family and Mr. Bennie, I believe she'll get over it."

Kim nodded. She believed that, as well. She felt herself being pulled closer into Duan's arms and then he leaned down and kissed her in a long, deep and devouring kiss. A part of her wished it could last forever, and that what was between them could last forever, as well, but she knew it wasn't meant to be. He had his life and she had hers. She would pursue her dream of becoming a doctor.

He finally broke off the kiss and tucked her body against his, but not before his lips skimmed hers once more. When she yawned, he smiled. "You're tired. Go on to sleep. I'll call you tomorrow from Atlanta."

Kim heard Duan say a few more words before the warmth of his body, the calmness of his voice and the tender kisses he was placing on her face compelled her to close her eyes and drift off to sleep. It was a good sleep. A restful sleep in the arms of the man she loved.

DUAN CONTINUED TO LIE there and hold Kim long after she had drifted off to sleep. More than anything he wanted to spend the rest of his life with her. Loving her and giving her every single thing she needed. But he knew that wasn't possible. Her life was already mapped out the way she wanted it. The dream she'd given up before was within her reach. So it was just as well that they ended things now, on a good note.

The tightening around his heart couldn't be helped. All he had to do was close his eyes and remember all the good times they'd shared. A part of him wanted to wake her up so they could make love one last time, but he knew that wouldn't happen.

He eased from the bed and headed toward the door. But before he could get there he turned around. That same tightening had moved to his throat. He wondered if she would remember the words of love that he'd spoken as she'd drifted off to sleep. Probably not. It was for the best.

He forced himself to turn and walk out the room. And with every step he told himself that ending things this way was the right thing to do.

WHEN KIM AWAKENED hours later she glanced out the window to see it was dark outside and the house was quiet. The ceiling light in the hallway illuminated her luggage letting her know Duan had brought it from the hotel.

She eased off the bed and left the room to go check on her mother. Wynona seemed to be in a peaceful sleep. Kim hoped that it was.

She left her mother's room and went into the kitchen. Duan had used some of her mother's fresh vegetables to make a soup and it smelled delicious. It was then that she saw the note he had scribbled and left on the counter.

Take care of yourself and Ms. Wynona.
Duan.

Kim swallowed the lump in her throat. This was his way of saying goodbye. He wasn't coming back. She had dreamed that he'd held her and told her he loved her, but she knew it had only been a dream.

She glanced around the kitchen and was almost overwhelmed in misery, but fought it back. She needed all her strength and energy to get her mother through this. It wasn't about her own heartbreak and pain; it was about her mother's.

Kim knew she was a fighter. She had a great future looming ahead of her. Medical school was within her reach. She would continue her life just the way she had before Duan entered into it.

She would survive and she would pursue and achieve her dreams. A part of her hoped and prayed that doing so would be enough.

17

"DUAN? WHY AREN'T YOU going to Sherri's birthday party in the Keys next weekend?"

For a long time Duan didn't say anything. He just stared across his office at his sister, wishing he could ignore the question. But he knew Olivia well enough to know she would hound him until he came up with what she considered a good answer. Married life had definitely made her bossier.

"I'm working on a case that requires my full concentration, Libby," he said, knowing that wasn't true. The case he was working on wasn't going to be that difficult to solve. What was difficult was giving it his full concentration.

"And before you ask, the answer is no," he said. "I haven't told Terrence I won't be coming, but I will. In fact I plan to call him later today."

He knew Libby's concern. As kids growing up they'd always shared their birthdays together and had made them special. Even when Libby lived in Paris, it was easy to do since she came home for the holidays and her birthday was two days before Christmas. And since Sherri, Reggie and Cathy were now official members of the Jeffries family, it was expected that everyone be present for their birthday celebrations, as well.

His sister crossed the room and placed her hands on his desk, looking directly into his eyes. "A difficult case has never stopped you before, Duan, so what's going on?"

He forced himself to maintain a pleasant expression. Otherwise, his sister, who didn't miss much when it came to her brothers, would see the pain lurking deep in his eyes. "Nothing's going on," he said, picking up a folder and making a pretense of browsing through it.

"You sure?"

He met her gaze again. "Yes, I'm sure." He glanced at his watch. "I thought you said you were on your lunch break."

She smiled as she leaned back. "When you're the boss, you can take a few liberties."

Duan knew he couldn't very well disagree with that. For a wedding gift, Reggie had purchased his wife an art gallery and a building to house it in a perfect location in Atlanta. Reggie had had the building remodeled to her specifications and *Libby's*—Olivia had chosen the name—was doing extremely well.

"Besides, I had a doctor's appointment."

He raised a concerned brow. "You're doing okay?"

She smiled. "Nothing eight months won't cure. Reggie and I are having a baby."

Duan blinked a few times to let her words fully sink in. A huge smile spread across his face and he pushed his chair back to stand. "Come here, sport."

When she came around his desk he pulled her into his arms. His little sister was going to be a mother, and he knew without a doubt that she would do a better job at it than their own mother had done.

"I'm sure Reggie knows already," he said, releasing her with a big grin. "Those damn Westmorelands believe in being fruitful and replenishing the Earth."

Olivia threw her head back and laughed. "Reggie actually knew before I did. We did the at-home pregnancy test a week ago, but the visit to the doctor today made it official. He was there with me when the doctor confirmed everything. Senator Reginald Westmoreland is definitely a happy man."

Duan nodded as he sat on the edge of his desk. "What about Dad and Terrence?"

"Dad knows and of course he and Cathy are delighted to become grandparents. I haven't told Terrence yet. I plan to call him and Sherri tonight."

She glanced down at her watch. "I better go since I do have an appointment at three with an artist whose work we want to display."

After his sister left, Duan wasn't able to get back to work. He leaned back in his chair and stared out the window. It had rained earlier but now the sun was out. Everywhere flowers were blooming, typical for May.

It had been three weeks since he had left Shreveport, and although he had spoken to Kim twice since then, that hadn't been enough. He knew her mother's outlook on life was improving, and that Mr. Bennie had stated his intentions to Wynona. The two adults were taking things one day at a time as they moved from friends to a more serious relationship. Duan had sent a bouquet of flowers to Wynona last week for Mother's Day, and she had called and left a message on his cell phone thanking him.

He knew Kim had told her mother and family the truth about their fake engagement. She had returned the ring to him a couple of weeks ago with a note thanking him for all he'd done. She'd also written that the family was so concerned about her mother's well-being that they hadn't dwelled on the fact that she'd lied to them.

The last time they talked he had told her that Villarosas had been charged in connection to his wives' deaths and was waiting trial. Villarosas still wasn't remorseful for what he'd done to his two wives and was trying to convince anyone who would listen that he had valid reasons for his actions.

When Duan had gotten the ring back he had stared at it remembering the exact moment he had placed it on Kim's finger. He'd been tempted to send it back to her and tell her to keep it since it looked as if it belonged on her hand. He still might do so, but knowing Kim, she would only return it.

Thanks to information he pulled from Terrence, he knew Kim had returned to the Keys and was back at work. He also knew the main reason he wouldn't be going to Sherri's birthday party: he wasn't ready to see her again. He wasn't sure if he could look at her and pretend not to want her and love her. So he had made the decision not to make the trip to Key West next weekend, and as he had told Libby, he would call Terrence and explain things.

Deciding that now was as good a time as any, he reached over and picked up the phone.

KIM GLANCED AROUND when she walked into Club Hurricane. Terrence was expecting her. Sherri's birthday party was coming up and he'd enlisted her help to make it special. The huge celebration would be held here at the club and Terrence had put her in charge of decorations.

"Hello, Ms. Cannon." Debbie, one of the club's hostesses, greeted her with a friendly smile on her face.

"Hi, Debbie. Is Terrence in? I believe he's expecting me, although I never told him what time I could make it. Working E.R. makes that impossible."

"Yes, I understand, and he said to send you right on up to his office whenever you arrived."

"Thanks." Kim headed into an elevator and leaned against the back panel. She checked her watch and saw it was a little past three in the afternoon. Since she had come straight from work she still wearing her nurse's scrubs.

She allowed her thoughts to drift to a subject she'd been trying to avoid thinking about and failing miserably. Duan. It had been three weeks since she'd seen him, three weeks since he had held her in his arms and kissed her with a passion that only he could deliver. And there was not a single day that went by that she didn't think of him and remember the time they'd spent together.

She had talked to him a few times when he'd called to see how she was doing and to check on her mother. But their conversations seemed rushed. He was afraid she would say something related to their time together and he hadn't wanted that. She had accepted that what they'd shared had meant more to her than it had to him and she'd moved on. At least she was trying to. The only thing she still had to do was decide which medical school she wanted to attend in the fall since several more offers had come in.

And she had finally been able to move beyond the issues she'd had with her father, although she was taking things one step at a time. After hearing about what had happened to her mother after Edward's arrest made national news, he had shown up in Shreveport while she was there.

Louis Cannon's appearance had drastically improved since she'd last seen him, and she could tell he was trying to take control of his life. He'd shared with both her and her mother that he hadn't taken a drink in over three years and was active in his church and had remarried. She was happy for him.

And she was also happy for her mother, who now had Mr. Bennie in her life. They, too, were taking things one step at a time. But Kim was convinced Mr. Bennie was the person her mother needed.

The elevator came to a stop and the door opened. Immediately, she could hear Terrence talking in a loud voice to someone on the speakerphone. She had taken a few steps toward his door when she recognized the voice of the person Terrence was conversing with. And when Terrence said her name, Kim stopped walking and listened.

"Hey, man, I hear what you're saying but I think you're wrong for not letting Kim know how you feel."

"I couldn't do that," Duan said in a voice filled with anguish. "I couldn't tell her that I love her so much I ache inside just thinking about her. She wants to go to med school. She's always wanted to go and someone took that dream away from her once. I won't be the one to take it away from her again."

"She can still go to med school, Duan. That's all I'm saying. When two people love each other, they can work through anything. The two of you can even have a long-distance relationship."

"She tried that before with a guy and it didn't work out so that's not an option. Besides, I'm not even sure she feels the same way about me. Our time together may not have meant as much to her as it meant to me. She never gave me any indication that she loved me."

Duan paused for a moment before continuing. "Look, Terrence, I didn't call to lay all this on you. It's my problem. I just wanted you to know the reason why I won't be coming to Sherri's birthday party next weekend. There is no way I can see Kim and not give away how much I want her. How much I love her. And I hope you understand."

Tears clouded Kim's eyes as she began backing away from Terrence's office door. She returned to the elevator and pressed the button that would take her back down. Her heart began filling with happiness at the thought that Duan loved her. All those times they *had* been making love and not just having sex. He actually loved her and wasn't telling her for fear of coming between her and her dream of attending medical school.

Didn't he know he was now part of her dream and that she had a chance to have it all with him? Apparently not. So she intended to be the one to tell him and she wouldn't waste any time doing so.

"You're through with your meeting with Terrence already?"

Kim blinked, realizing the elevator door had opened and Debbie was standing in front of it, staring at her.

"Oh, no. I just got an emergency that I need to take care of. Let Terrence know I'll call him later to reschedule our meeting."

"All right."

Kim quickly headed for the exit door, pulling her car keys out of her purse. She would drive herself to the airport. Destination? Atlanta, Georgia.

18

DUAN RECALLED the conversation he'd had with Terrence before leaving the office. Maybe his brother was right and he should let Kim know how he felt.

To anyone who didn't know Duan, he probably appeared to be a calm, cool and collected guy. A man defined by his achievements, someone who knew what he wanted and was proud of what he had. A man not willing to show his emotions to too many people. A private person. Definitely not a man who would bare his soul to anyone. And Duan could admit that before he'd met Kim, that image was probably right on the money.

But now he was also a man who knew how it felt to love a woman, truly love a woman. Now he understood his father's tears that day. He understood the pain of loving someone and not having that love returned. Although he was certain the depth of his father's misery was deeper than his because of his wife's betrayal, the bottom line was that love was love no matter how you looked at it. And he could admit that he was a man in love. And the sad thing was that the woman who had his heart didn't have a clue.

He headed toward the kitchen to prepare one of those microwave dinners when his doorbell rang. He pivoted, wondering who the hell it could be. He wasn't in a good mood and the last thing he wanted was company.

Without bothering to glance out the peephole, he flung open the door, ready to give the person hell for having the nerve to bother him on a Thursday night.

His breath caught in his throat and he felt himself stagger back a foot. He blinked, thinking he was seeing things, and when he realized he wasn't, he asked in a shocked voice, "Kim, what are you doing here?"

She smiled and that smile did something to him that he couldn't explain, and all the frustration and anger he'd felt earlier seemed to melt away. "I was wondering, Duan, if you wanted to play."

DUAN BLINKED AGAIN, but when he fully realized what she'd asked, he reached out and pulled her into his arms, covering his mouth with hers. He then swept her off her feet and slammed the door shut with his foot.

He had a vague memory of Kim tossing her purse on his sofa. But what stood out in his mind more than anything was when he carried her into his bedroom and proceeded to strip her naked before tearing off his own clothes, popping buttons in his haste.

Oh, yeah, they would play. Then afterward they would talk.

He glanced over at her and almost had an orgasm right then and there. She was propped back on his pillows in that sexy, mouth-watering pose he liked. Her legs were open, showing him everything, and her scent was driving him insane. It was definitely an aphrodisiac moment.

He moved toward her but thought he needed to make one thing clear right now. "We're not having sex, Kim."

She smiled. "We're not?"

"No."

"Then what is it that we're about to do?"

"Make love," he quickly replied.

His knee touched the mattress of the bed and he reached out for her. Pulling her closer to him, he whispered against her lips, "I could never just have sex with the woman I love."

There, he'd said it, and he hoped and prayed Terrence was right, that maybe, quite possibly, things could work out between them and that she cared for him, too.

She rose up on her knees and wrapped her arms around his neck. He dragged in a deep breath at the feel of her hard nipples pressed into his chest. She held his gaze, flicking out her tongue a few times to trace the outline of his lips before saying, "That's good to hear, Duan, because you're the man I love."

At that moment everything within Duan snapped and he grabbed the back of her neck and lowered his mouth to hers, devouring her in a kiss that only the two of them could share. It was a kiss that let them know beyond a shadow of a doubt that no matter what, they belonged together and they *would* be together.

He took his time to cherish every part of her body, loving her, tasting her and transforming her into sexual energy in his arms. And when he lowered his head between her thighs and gently parted her folds with his fingers, he eased his tongue inside and began stroking her all the way to the tip of her clit, darting in and out of her, lapping her with a hunger that was consuming him. She screamed out his name and reached down to grab hold of his head to push his tongue even deeper inside her. Giving him more of her taste. More of her as an orgasm ripped through her body.

Before her climax could ease away, he slid between those same open thighs and entered her, throwing his head back in a guttural groan at how good it felt being back inside her. And when he felt himself all the way to the hilt, he began moving in long, deep strokes, delving in and out, back and forth, mating with her, making love to her, making both their bodies tremble in what had to be the most precious pleasure any two individuals could share.

And when she screamed his name again, he knew he was about to follow her lead, and as everything erupted inside him, exploded to the nth degree, he shot his semen all the way to her womb.

"Kim!"

He screamed out the name of the woman he loved. The woman who had made him whole. The only woman he ever wanted to belong to. This woman. His woman. And then he busted another nut when an orgasm slammed into him again. He felt her inner muscles clench him, taking everything he had.

And when he had nothing left to give, he slumped down on her in mindless ecstatic pleasure and contentment.

"TELL ME, KIM. You knew, didn't you?"

A very drained Kim glanced up at the eyes staring down at her, the eyes of the man she loved. "Yes, but only recently," she responded in a strained whisper.

She saw the confusion enter his eyes. "But how…?"

"I had an appointment with Terrence after work today to go over his plans for Sherri's party, and when I stepped off the elevator I heard him talking to you. He had placed you on the speakerphone and I overheard what you said."

More confusion flashed in the dark depths of his eyes. "But that was just a couple of hours ago."

She smiled. "I know. Once I heard you say you loved me, but that you weren't sure I loved you, I knew I had to come here and tell you in person. So, without Terrence even knowing I'd been there, I left and drove directly to the airport."

A look of incredulity shone on Duan's face. "Without a ticket?"

Kim managed a chuckle. "A ticket was the least of my problems. I had to call to let the hospital know I wouldn't be in tomorrow. Luckily I was scheduled to be off this weekend anyway. But the biggest goof of all was when I discovered I didn't have a house address for you until I got in the cab and the driver asked where I was going. I had to call Sherri to get it."

Duan threw his head back and laughed.

She couldn't help but join in when she thought about it, although it hadn't been funny at the time. "So, I guess you can say that my visit here was rather spontaneous."

Duan grinned from ear to ear. "Yes, I think it would be safe to say that. *Spontaneous* is definitely the word of the day, and it seems the norm for us."

"And if you noticed, I was wearing my nurse's uniform, which means unless you plan to have me walking around nude all weekend, I'll need more clothes. And a few toiletries."

"You walking around naked won't be a problem for me," Duan informed her. "In fact I rather like the idea. And as for the toiletries, just make a list of everything you need and I'll go out and get them."

He reached out and rubbed the tip of his finger across her chin. "I meant what I said to Terrence, Kim. I won't stand in the way of your dream. You *are* going to med school."

The corners of her lips tilted into a smile. "Yes, I am going to medical school. But Terrence was right, Duan. You and I can work out anything because we love each other. I will go to med school, and on the flight here I decided which one, since I've received several offers. I'm going to accept the offer from Emory University here in Atlanta. That means you're going to have a roommate for a while, Duan Jeffries."

Kim scrutinized his face to see how the thought of her moving in with him would go over, especially when she would be unemployed and going to school full-time. From the smile on his face, she knew he was fine with the idea.

"I would love for you to share this place with me, Kim," he said, leaning closer to her. "But only as a short-term roommate."

He reached in the drawer to the nightstand behind him and pulled out a small box. Kim recognized it immediately. It was his grandmother's ring. The ring she had returned to him a few weeks ago. The ring she had grown used to wearing. The one she'd fallen in love with. The ring that looked perfect on her hand.

Tears filled her eyes as he took her hand in his. "I'd rather have you as my wife instead of a roommate. Kim, will you marry me? Be the mother of our babies? Trust me to make you happy? And know that on the day you become Dr. Kimani Cannon Jeffries, I will be just as happy as you, and that I will cherish you, honor you and forever love you."

Kim smiled and raised her eyebrows. "And will you play with me anytime I want?"

He chuckled. "Yes, sweetheart, I will play with you anytime you want."

"In that case, yes, I will marry you."

Duan slid the ring on her finger and leaned down and kissed her with all the longing and hunger of a man in love. When he finally pulled back she smiled up at him, placed her arms around his neck, and said, "I'm ready to play some more."

And they did.

* * * * *

Kay Young returned to woozy consciousness to find that she was lying on a soft sofa beneath a heap of quilts near a cheerfully burning fire. When she tried to move, however, everything hurt, and she groaned.

At once she heard a sound, then a stranger with a hard, harsh face was squatting beside her. "Shh," he said softly. "You're safe here. I promise."

"I have to go," she said weakly, struggling against pain. "He'll find me. He can't find me."

"Easy, lady," he said quietly. "You're hurt. No one's going to find you here."

"He will," she said desperately, terror clutching at her insides. "He always finds me!"

"Easy," he said again. "There's a blizzard outside. No one's getting here tonight, not even the doctor. I know, because I tried."

"Doctor? I don't need a doctor! I've got to get away."

"There's nowhere to go tonight," he said levelly. "And if I thought you could stand, I'd take you to a window and show you."

But even as she tried once more to pull away the quilts, she remembered something else: this man had been gentle when he'd found her beside the road, even when she had kicked and clawed. He hadn't hurt her.

Terror receded just a bit. She looked at him and detected signs of true concern there.

The terror eased another notch and she let her head sag on the pillow. "He always finds me," she whispered.

"Not here. Not tonight. That much I can guarantee."

Will Kay's mysterious rescuer protect her
from her worst fears?
Find out in HER HERO IN HIDING
by New York Times *bestselling author Rachel Lee.*
Available June 2010, only from
Silhouette® Romantic Suspense.

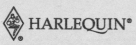

LAURA MARIE ALTOM

The Baby Twins

Stephanie Olmstead has her hands full raising
her twin baby girls on her own. When she runs
into old friend Brady Flynn, she's shocked to find
herself suddenly attracted to the handsome airline
pilot! Will this flyboy be the perfect daddy—
or will he crash and burn?

"LOVE, HOME & HAPPINESS"

www.eHarlequin.com

HAR75309

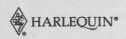

HARLEQUIN®

Showcase

Reader favorites from the most talented voices in romance

Save $1.00 on the purchase of 1 or more Harlequin® Showcase books.

On sale May 11, 2010

- -

SAVE $1.00

on the purchase of 1 or more Harlequin® Showcase books.

Coupon expires Oct 31, 2010. Redeemable at participating retail outlets.
Limit one coupon per purchase. Valid in the U.S.A. and Canada only.

52609015

Canadian Retailers: Harlequin Enterprises Limited will pay the face value of this coupon plus 10.25¢ if submitted by customer for this product only. Any other use constitutes fraud. Coupon is nonassignable. Void if taxed, prohibited or restricted by law. Consumer must pay any government taxes. Void if copied. Nielsen Clearing House ("NCH") customers submit coupons and proof of sales to Harlequin Enterprises Limited, P.O. Box 3000, Saint John, NB E2L 4L3, Canada. Non-NCH retailer—for reimbursement submit coupons and proof of sales directly to Harlequin Enterprises Limited, Retail Marketing Department, 225 Duncan Mill Rd., Don Mills, ON M3B 3K9, Canada.

U.S. Retailers: Harlequin Enterprises Limited will pay the face value of this coupon plus 8¢ if submitted by customer for this product only. Any other use constitutes fraud. Coupon is nonassignable. Void if taxed, prohibited or restricted by law. Consumer must pay any government taxes. Void if copied. For reimbursement submit coupons and proof of sales directly to Harlequin Enterprises Limited, P.O. Box 880478, El Paso, TX 88588-0478, U.S.A. Cash value 1/100 cents.

5 65373 00076 2   (8100)0 11651

® and TM are trademarks owned and used by the trademark owner and/or its licensee.
© 2009 Harlequin Enterprises Limited

HSCCOUP0410

Silhouette Desire

From *USA TODAY* bestselling author

LEANNE BANKS

CEO'S EXPECTANT SECRETARY

Elle Linton is hiding more than just her affair
with her boss Brock Maddox. And she's
terrifed that if their secret turns public her
mother's life may be put at risk. When she
unexpectedly becomes pregnant she's forced
to make a decision. Will she be able to save
her relationship and her mother's life?

Available June
wherever books are sold.

Always Powerful, Passionate and Provocative.

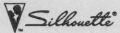

REQUEST YOUR FREE BOOKS!

2 FREE NOVELS PLUS 2 FREE GIFTS!

HARLEQUIN®

Blaze

Red-hot reads!

HB10R

HARLEQUIN® *Blaze*™

is proud to present

New York Times bestselling author

Vicki Lewis Thompson

with a brand-new trilogy,
SONS OF CHANCE
**where three sexy brothers
meet three irresistible women.**

Look for the first book
WANTED!

*Available beginning in June 2010
wherever books are sold.*

---

red-hot reads